CRAVE

BRAWLERS

J.M. DABNEY

DEDICATION

To the ones who wanted to meet the Brawlers.

AUTHOR'S NOTE

Although this is part of a series Crave is a complete stand alone.

Trigger Warning: This title deals with past abuse, self-harm, and suicide.

CONTENTS

1 SADLY ALL HIS BRAINS WERE IN HIS DICK

Chaos reigned at Brawlers Bar. Fists flew from every direction and bodies fell against Crave Butler. He was about to spin to take on the guy at his six but pulled the punch at the last moment as Bull his coworker came into view.

"Motherfucker, are all your brains in your fucking dick," Bull growled.

He protested, "This wasn't my fault." He ruined the innocent tone as he laughed like a maniac.

He hadn't thrown the first fucking punch, so actually, he wasn't lying. Bodies started flying up and out of the crowd as he spotted Psycho tossing people around like they weighed nothing. Almost seven-feet of pissed off man was downright fucking Scary; no way in fuck he'd admit that to anyone, though.

Then the realization came. Shit, Psycho was after him. He started to duck and weave, disappearing for someone Crave's size was impossible. He lifted weights at least three times a week, he was the shortest of Brawlers Security team at six-two but other than Psycho he was definitely the bulkiest in muscle mass.

"Elijah is fine," he yelled and tried to hide behind Bull.

"I told you no fights when my pretty boss is in-house."

Crave rolled his eyes, he swore Psycho had a massive hard-on for Elijah. If true, Psycho had a death wish.

"Scary and Tank—"

"Not my bosses. Now, come here so I can kick your ass."

"Bull, do something." Crave peeked over Bull's shoulder. "The fucker is insane."

"Just take it like a man, Crave." Bull walked away.

Crave was exposed. "Come on, man, I didn't throw—"

He ducked a right jab but grunted when a left hook landed against his ribs "Motherfucker, are you wearing brass?" The question ceased when huge hands grabbed his shoulders and pushed him down. Psycho's knee came toward his nose in slow motion. He barely pushed himself out of the way, and the worn denim of Psycho's jeans grazed his cheek.

"Psycho," Elijah's raised voice came out of nowhere.

He turned his head in time to see Elijah with his hands on his hips and a dark brow raised.

"Yes, boss?"

"What are you doing?"

"Kicking Crave's ass."

Crave rolled his eyes as he took advantage of Psycho's distraction and tried to pull away only to earn himself a sucker punch to the gut. The air whooshed from his lungs as he planted his hands on his knees and tried to draw in a breath.

"And why are you kicking Crave's ass?"

"Because he didn't listen to me," Psycho answered.

"Is that a question or an answer?"

"Um, it's an answer, he didn't listen and put you in danger."

Crave snorted. Elijah might be lacking in muscle and height, but the man could wield a mean bat when the time arose.

"I was perfectly safe, Psycho, what have we talked about?"

"Don't beat up on people weaker than—"

Elijah had the nerve to laugh. Bastard.

"No, what did we discuss?"

"To think before we punch, but I thought about it. And after careful consideration, he deserved the beating."

"Psycho."

The big bastard exhaled heavily and hung his head.

"We don't fight with friends. He's not my friend."

"Psycho, come on, let's have another talk, come on." Elijah held out his hand.

Crave straightened and earned an elbow to the gut. "Dammit."

"Psycho, no, bad Psycho, are we going to have to talk about another visit to the doctor?"

Psycho huffed and Crave watched him walk away.

"No, boss, I'm—" Psycho growled, then cleared his throat, "Sorry."

"Shouldn't you tell Crave you're sorry too?"

"Do I have'ta?"

"No, but we still have to talk, buy me a coffee."

Elijah was insane, he'd thought it when the cute man hooked up with his bosses Tank and Scary, but when he adopted Psycho, it turned into a fact. The small man slipped his arm through Psycho's and led him away. Crave breathed a sigh of relief and jumped back as a massive fist came back to pop him in the nuts.

"Dude, that's low."

"What did you do?"

"Nothing, boss."

Psycho smirked over his shoulder as he walked away with Elijah on his arm.

"Your boss won't always be around to save your ass," Crave called out and grimaced as he ducked away as Psycho tried to turn back to him.

"He's gonna kill you one of these days."

Scary's gruff voice made him turn his head to see his boss's amused expression.

"Why haven't you fired his oversized ass yet?"

"Elijah loves that man like a son, which is weird as fuck since the man is only a year younger than him."

"Does he join—"

"I'll kick your ass if you finish that shit right there. I don't know what the fuck is going on with you, but you cause one more fight in my bar, I'll let Psycho kick your ass to the door. Got me?"

"Sorry, man, I shouldn't have said that."

"Damn right," Scary growled and headed toward where Elijah and Psycho were sitting at the bar.

Fuck, Crave slid his hands into his back pockets and watched as Bull cleared the mess. Setting some of Psycho's casualties up with a free round. He probably deserved the beating Elijah saved him from, but he probably needed one from Scary too. Crave lived with a constant inappropriate comment fighting to get free from his mouth. He knew it, and mostly he didn't give a fuck if it got him in trouble, but he knew better than to try his shit with Scary. That mean fucker would hide his body and never think twice.

Scanning the crowd, he noticed most of the rowdy crowd departed. He made his way outside to take his usual spot on a barstool beside the door.

He stared out across the parking lot to the deputy vehicle in the empty lot on the other side of the road. He gave the guy a two-finger salute, and the deputy flashed his headlights. The new guy seemed cool enough. He didn't fuck with them as much as the others did.

He yelled as a bag of ice slammed into his sore stomach. "What the fuck, man." Crave turned his head to find Twitch standing next to him. The man tucked his long curls behind his small ears and crossed his arms over his thin chest. Crave never met a man he'd consider beautiful before, but that ended the minute Twitch sashayed into Brawlers for an interview.

"You pissed off the bosses again."

"Don't fucking start, Twitch."

"I'm not starting anything. Just saying."

"Am I fired?"

They'd threatened to fire him before and with any other job he'd taken he hadn't given a shit about it, but he loved working there.

"They finally have a solid crew they trust, but whatever's going on in that head of yours, you better work it out before they change their minds."

It's like none of them knew him. He was the same as he was the minute he'd walked into Brawlers. Eight years he'd worked the door of Brawlers as second in command to Tank. Like the rest of the crew except the bosses, he'd taken up residence in Bull's house. They lived and worked together sooner or later shit was going to get tense, they'd fight and be done. He had to admit his head was fucked up lately. Crave remembered the minute shit went fucking nuclear—Twitch had smiled at him.

"I ain't got shit going on in my head," he lied like a motherfucker. "And I didn't throw the first punch."

"You rarely do, but you sure as hell don't back down."

"Kinda my job."

"I'm going back inside, Hunter isn't screwing up my paperwork again. How fucking hard is it to learn the POS?"

Twitch didn't wait for him to answer and headed back through the open door. Crave dropped the bag of ice to the ground. He hadn't gotten laid in almost a year, and it was all Twitch's fault. His usual type was a big and muscular, but submissive.

Twitch was too fragile for him, yet he didn't want anyone else. Okay, he hadn't turned into a monk since he'd first laid eyes on Twitch. The unfamiliar guilt he had over the men he'd brought home or hooked up with caused him to hook up infrequently until it ceased completely last summer. He loved sex. Fuck, he just missed fucking, but he only wanted one man.

He'd wanted to touch Twitch's smooth tanned skin and trace every inch of that beautiful slim body from the second Crave had spotted him. Crave dreamed of tangling Twitch's long dark hair around his fist as he fucked Twitch's tight, rounded ass till Twitch screamed for him. He wanted to own Twitch; the man's pleasure and pain all his.

Crave didn't understand the concept of jealousy and didn't become attached, but every man who even looked at Twitch got a warning. With his size, they never went against him, and he made sure they knew he wasn't fucking around.

He wouldn't share his boy, and every motherfucker knew it; if they didn't, they learned quickly and painfully.

"No more fighting tonight," Bull's deep, gravelly voice jolted him out of his thoughts.

"I'm not—"

"I know that look, and it's never good."

Crave shot a glance at the silver haired man and found Bull's glare promising retribution. Bull had worked there even longer than him. He called the grumpy bastard one of his best friends, but Bull wasn't a man to fuck with no matter how long they'd been friends.

"I've gotten enough shit, Bull."

"Listen, we don't fight amongst ourselves. That shit is for the ring, remember it."

Oh, he remembered, he'd tangled with Bull and Psycho, even Tank and Scary a few times. At Bull's they settled arguments in the boxing ring Bull had set up in the barn. When the fight ended, they left it on the mat.

"Psycho came after me."

"I already talked to him. This shit won't keep happening. I ain't the parent here."

"I got it, no need—"

"Definitely a need since you threatened that fucker because he flirted with Twitch. Don't try to deny it because I saw you smile when he threw the punch. I ain't saying nothing about it, but either you take care of claiming your boy, or you let him go."

Again he wasn't given a chance to respond, and Bull disappeared.

His secret was out, fuck. Hopefully Bull would keep it to himself. There was only so much he could take from his co-workers and friends. He had to live with these people, even Twitch took up residence in what became known as Brawlers Farm.

His control was slim on a good day, nonexistent any other time. Crave already caught Twitch sneaking out on several nights over the past couple of months. He was positive there was someone out there he couldn't threaten. Some strange man putting his hands on Twitch—fucking Twitch. The beautiful man didn't know it yet but Crave owned him. His fists clenched so hard his knuckles cracked. He growled low in his chest and caused two men leaving to jump. He didn't apologize, something in their retreat satisfied him.

He just had to find Twitch's boyfriend, destroy the motherfucker, and prove to Twitch Crave was the man for him. Easy, right?

2 TWITCH NEEDED IT LIKE AIR TO BREATHE

Classical music softly played in the background. The dinner table impeccably designed down the intricate plate and glass folds of the linen napkins. Twitch Harrison straightened his spine, squared his shoulders, and pretended he wasn't getting ready to lose his shit. As with any invite to his childhood home for dinner, he waited for the first verbal strike. By the end of the visit, Weston and Caroline would expertly reduce him to choked back tears.

He stared down at the perfectly plated meal. Twitch knew he'd have to force down some of the food on his plate, but the thought of eating caused his stomach to revolt. Why did he continue to subject himself to his mother and father's summons?

The second he walked through the door of the house, memories he'd rather forget assailed him from the back of his mind. Twitch attempted yet frequently failed to ignore them. He'd barely turned twelve the first time his father sent him away. His father said the religious retreat would rid him of his sinful desires. Twitch had survived months of torture over the next four years. Numerous stays during school breaks and every time he returned home, the bullying from his classmates were tame in comparison.

Twitch couldn't hide what and who he was, he'd lost count of the times he'd tried. Being born turned into the first failure of many. He'd come into the world almost three months early. By rights, Twitch shouldn't even be alive. At thirteen, he'd attempted suicide for the first time, then again the following two years.

The righteous religious men who ran the so-called therapy retreats beat him while spouting Scripture, electrocuted him until the only safe sensations for him were pain. He twined his fingers together and squeezed to keep himself from skimming the scars hidden under the expensive linen of his dress shirt. Six months passed since he'd last taken a razor to his flesh.

Each visit made it harder to resist. If he cried, he needed the pain. If he experienced pleasure, he needed the pain to drive it away. The farm and Brawlers were the only places he'd attained a semblance of normalcy and safety. He just wanted to go home.

"We're having the Merriweathers visit next month," His father's cool, crisp tone drew him from his thoughts.

Twitch knew what would come. The Merriweather family came from old money and had a beautiful daughter. His parents denied the fact he'd come out, worked in a gay bar, and couldn't attempt a façade of passing. Their philosophy, if they didn't speak of it, then it didn't exist.

"I thought they'd settled in France after Milton took over the company."

"They did, but Alicia is graduating, I believe you…"

He tuned it out. Yes, he knew Alicia, and her level of entitlement had astounded him the first time he'd met her. His parents took the opportunity to push them together every chance. All in the name of business and connections. There'd been much more before her.

Mother and father didn't care he was gay if he didn't act on it. Not that he had much choice; sex pushed him into panic attacks. Hell, he was twenty-five and never been kissed. What could pathetically compare to that? *Being in love with a man he could never have.*

They insisted he did his duty. Repent and find a wife, have kids and deny everything he'd fought every day to attain.

"Evan, pay attention."

He snapped his focus back to his parents, and their disapproval choked him. His mother's lips were pursed, but other than that there wasn't any expression, her perfectly applied makeup downplayed her prominent Asian features. He'd taken after her more than his father. His father was broad, a man who demanded respect by his presence alone.

As he sometimes did, he searched them for any sign that they loved him and he didn't find any sentiment toward him whatsoever. They frowned on affection. Emotion was as unacceptable as blasphemy. The Good Book was law in the Harrison House.

"I'm sorry."

"We've arranged for Alicia and you to spend some time together. Make sure you don't disappoint us."

Wasn't that the problem: his sin. Twitch just wanted to go home to the farm; just be somewhere people loved him. He raised his hand and reached for his fork, he took a bite and pretended he wasn't going to throw up.

....

Hours later, Twitch paced his room with his keys cupped in his palms. The edges cut into his palms as he obsessively checked the time. Only an hour past since he'd heard the last noise of everyone settling in for the night. His backpack felt heavy, and he swore every board under his feet creaked as he made his way to his door.

His heart hammered a panicked rhythm in his chest. Twitch was a grown ass man at twenty-five, but he was terrified of getting caught sneaking out. He lowered his right hand to the brass knob and pressed his keys to his chest with the other. He took one deep breath, then held it as he slowly turned it and started opening the door.

He flinched as it creaked and stopped, he listened for someone coming. When he was satisfied he hadn't alerted anyone, he pulled it open enough to slip his thin body through the crack. Why did he have to be like that? He'd already taken more of his anxiety meds than prescribed, but he needed it. An afternoon and early evening with his parents always drove him over the edge.

His world was always tilting on its axis. He closed the door and listened to the faint click of the lock. Luckily his room was on the first floor of the farmhouse. If he had to deal with the steps, Twitch would freak out the rest of the way. All he wanted was security, and he'd found one place where it was acceptable for him to break.

He reached out to open the front door, but a throat clearing caused him to jump, then pivot on his toes to press his back against the wall. A huge shadow took up the doorway into the kitchen.

"Going somewhere," Crave's deep rumbling timbre practically boomed in the darkness.

Shit, shit, shit, shit! Twitch chewed nervously on his bottom lip and held tighter on the fist full of keys until he felt them cut into the soft hollow of his palm. The pain bringing him slightly back to focus. No, he couldn't do the pain anymore. He needed something more; he'd replaced the cutting with something else.

"Um, just going out for a drive. I couldn't sleep, what are you still doing up?"

"You do a lot of drives lately."

Crave's accusatory tone made him flinch in the darkness, and he hoped Crave didn't notice.

He bit the inside of his cheek, dammit, he had to stop. No pain, no pain, fuck, it was getting bad. He needed to leave and soon. He eased his left hand back, the metal cool in his hand as he started to turn it.

"Stop," Crave ordered.

Twitch squeaked and froze.

"Who is he?"

"Who?" Twitch's confusion grew at the anger in Crave's voice.

Even when Crave fought, he never appeared angry. The man enjoyed the violence too much. Crave always smiled, but his eyes gave him away. Although, in the dark, Twitch couldn't get a read on him.

He'd always been able to tell when someone was angry with him; when they were ready to strike. Twitch closed his eyes as he tried to focus and bring his breathing under control. He wouldn't embarrass himself by hyperventilating in front of anyone, especially Crave.

"Who're you fucking, only reason to sneak out, someone you met—"

"I'm not fucking anyone," Twitch answered, and his voice rose several octaves.

"Why are you fucking lying?"

"I'm not."

Crave moved in his direction, and Twitch pressed closer to the door. His face started burning at the sound of his whimpers. Weak, that's what he was.

"Don't—"

Twitch threw open the door and spun to dart through the door. He ran through the darkness to his car. His hands shook as he pressed the button on the fob to unlock the doors. He ignored the roar of Crave's voice as the man called his name. The keys almost fell from his shaking hands. He finally made it into the driver's seat and slammed the door, locking them.

"Come on, come on," He repeated as it took him three tries to get the key into the ignition and even longer to get the car started.

Sweat made his shirt stick to his back. He darted a glance toward the house to find Crave standing on the steps. He pulled out too fast and sent gravel flying behind him. Twitch drove toward town with his mind in chaos and losing his focus, his calm.

Crave had seen what he truly was, the broken man he'd tried to hide behind sarcasm and quick laughter. He turned off before reaching the *Welcome to Powers* sign and took the long drive toward the only place he could ground himself. He knew he'd wear out his welcome soon, but until Twitch did, he was going to take advantage of his friends understanding and compassion.

The porch light was like a beacon, and he quickly reached the parking spot next to Lucky's car. Priest and Lucky invited him to stay the night six months ago, and had done so once a week since.

He got out of his vehicle, then closed and locked the door.

His legs shook as he took slow even steps until he noticed the front door open and Lucky stood framed there. His pet rat Plague perched on his shoulder.

"Almost didn't think you were coming," Lucky said as he pushed open the screen door.

"Crave caught me."

"You okay," Lucky asked.

Twitch ducked under his arm and into the house, Priest instantly opened his arms. He couldn't resist the haven the man represented. They'd all talked on the nights he'd stayed about his past—what he was running from. Twitch stepped into Priest's arm and twined his own around Priest's waist. The softness and warmth exactly what he needed and he felt himself become grounded. His heart no longer a lump in his throat.

"Baby, why don't you get him settled in bed while I put Plague in his cage?"

It would probably seem weird to anyone who found out he spent nights sleeping in bed with his friends, but he wasn't attracted to either of them. Lucky and Priest were entirely devoted to each other. It was just nice to occasionally be included in that safety.

He sighed as he was led down the hall to the room at the end of it. A large four-poster bed set center stage with fabric cascading down the dark wood posts. The covers were already pushed down.

"You didn't answer Lucky's question, you okay," Priest asked.

The big man released him, then Priest slipped the backpack off Twitch's shoulders. He hadn't even realized he was still wearing it.

"It was so embarrassing, I almost had—"

"There's nothing to be ashamed of, and I don't want you to think there is."

"Why do you two put up with me?"

"Twitch, we love you. Lucky was there for me when I was at my lowest. We wouldn't even think of not doing the same for you. Did you—"

"No, I don't do that anymore, I promise."

"It's okay, calm down, you sleeping in that or—"

Twitch stepped to the edge of the bed and stripped down to his boy shorts. No one besides Lucky and Priest had seen him without his clothes since he was sixteen. It was the first time he'd taken a razor to his ribs. The scars were faded to almost white while others were still pink. It had been six months since he'd cut himself.

He crawled into the big bed and lay down in the middle. Priest leaned over and picked up Cyclops, the three-legged and one-eyed cat and settled her on his chest. The cat's loud purring and whiskers tickled his throat as she cuddled in.

"Maybe we should take you to the shelter to get a pet," Priest suggested as he climbed into bed on his right.

A yell made him laugh as Lucky took a running leap and bounced onto the bed. "Now, are my two favorite men ready to sleep, we're going to go see the baby in the morning." Lucky practically vibrated.

Priest and Lucky were expecting a baby by surrogate. Lou, Lucky's twin, offered them womb space. She said it was a one-time only deal.

"We find out the sex, want to come with us?"

"Can I," Twitched whispered.

"Yeah, don't think we haven't seen you talking to the baby almost as much as Lucky."

He wasn't able to answer—too afraid he'd start crying. These two men were his best friends. They'd included him in their lives and cuddled him when he felt lost. He didn't ever want to lose this.

"Okay, bedtime." Lucky wrapped them both in his arms.

The calm was instant, and Twitch closed his eyes, as he was sandwiched tightly between Priest and Lucky. The only thing still bothering him was Crave's anger. It wasn't the first time Crave was mad at him and probably wouldn't be the last. He took his job as Second to Head of Security seriously, and Twitch wasn't exactly Psycho or Bull. Twitch was five-foot-six, and a weak hundred-thirty pounds, he didn't have the muscle or skill to defend himself when shit went south at Brawlers.

He sighed as he snuggled in and tried to rid his head of Crave and what waited for him when he went home. Right then, he could sleep safe and content, once he got up, he could go see a baby for the first time. He finally drifted off with a smile on his face.

3 JUSTIFIABLE HOMICIDE

Crave clenched his fists so tight his knuckles popped. Twitch ran from him and to someone else. He tried to focus on the burn of the needle as it moved along his ribs. Trouble was leaned over finishing up the outline of Crave's new ink. His friend had shaken his head when Crave told him what he wanted. He didn't give a shit. He did what he wanted; when he wanted. Most of the time it got him in serious shit, but it was just a tattoo.

"Did you see how tiny he was," Twitch's animated voice followed the chime over the door.

Twitch sounded so fucking happy and Crave got even more pissed. Less than twelve hours ago, Twitch cowered in terror of him.

"So, we're finally getting a boy," Trouble asked, but never looked up.

"Yep, he had ten tiny toes and fingers, he was perfect. He looked like he was sucking his thumb. I got to feel—"

Twitch stopped talking and Crave finally looked toward him to find his man tucked under Lucky's arm. His slim hands fisted in the man's t-shirt. Twitch stared right at him and worried his bottom lip between his teeth.

"It took forever to get the gel off his hands because he kept following our son's kicks," Priest laughed as he spoke. "We'd get one clean and then have to take a wipe to the other."

Priest actually leaned down and kissed the top of Twitch's loose curls. Crave's fingers dug deeper into his palms.

"But he was so happy, baby, Lou even let Twitch have extra belly cuddle time. Our son is going to know his voice more than ours."

There was no heat in Lucky's voice. Lucky and Priest took Twitch under their wing almost two years ago. When Lucky was almost killed in a hit and run, at the hospital, he'd watched Twitch climb into bed between the two men and barely kept himself from killing them. No one touched what was his. He was such an asshole, at least he admitted it.

Was there more than friends between his two friends and Twitch?

"Calm the fuck down, Crave, shit," Trouble grumped, but never took his focus off his work.

"I'm calm."

"Yeah, right, sorry to tell you this, you don't hide your jealousy well."

"Who the fuck said I was jealous?"

"Even me who's not rocking full brain capacity can tell."

"He's been sneaking out at night to see them."

"You're crazy. Lucky and Priest are the poster couple for monogamy. They definitely ain't into a third or even an occasional threesome."

"Then why the fuck is my—"

"He's not yours. Done," Trouble announced.

Trouble wiped down his side with a paper towel and antiseptic.

"You know the routine, so I ain't gotta repeat it. We'll give it a few weeks, and you'll come back for color."

"Thanks, man, it looks great."

Crave held up his left arm and looked down at his side. The skin was red from hours of abuse and discolored from the black ink. He resisted the urge to touch it. To stroke the thin lines of the angel with long dark hair and wings wrapped around himself. Twitch.

He knew he was insane and surly, but Crave knew what he wanted. It was just a matter of getting the little man to agree to be his. At that point, he didn't see that happening anytime soon or at all.

"Why don't you talk to him? Ya know, doing the thing a normal partner would do."

Crave snarled. Talking wasn't Crave's strong suit. He was more a man of action. While he waited for Trouble to cover his ribs with plastic wrap he reached for his shirt.

Twitch was still talking a mile a minute, but he was perched on the reception desk making Zerk, Landon's husband, laugh. Landon's parents owned Twirled World Ink.

Twitch never spoke to him like that. Yeah, they talked, you couldn't work and live with someone for almost four years and not learn something about the person. Although, he realized he didn't know a lot about Twitch.

The man didn't talk about his past or what he did before he came back to Powers after leaving college. Twitch had barely turned twenty-one when he'd walked into Brawlers that first day for an interview. He'd worn a baggy pink t-shirt and jeans that hung on him. Twitch had had his long hair twisted into a messy bun at the nape of his long, elegant neck. His skin lightly tanned and dusted with the cutest freckles.

Crave swore his bosses would've sent the man packing, but they'd hired him. He'd started the next night. Twitch worked a bar like it was second nature. There wasn't a drink Twitch didn't know how to mix, and if the guys tried to stump him, he just came up with his own without batting his long lashes.

Also, he'd never seen someone talk a drunk down faster than Twitch could. All it took was a sweet smile and a soft touch. Crave hated those nights. Especially when those men took Twitch's gentle compassion for something more. Crave set them straight and fast.

He might give Twitch shit about it and other stuff, but everyone knew he was an asshole.

He just couldn't get the way Twitch acted earlier that morning out of his head. Twitch had curled his shoulders as if he were trying to make himself small and invisible. He wanted to know who'd done that to the man he wanted. Who'd caused that level of fear?

Crave slung his shirt over his shoulder and walked up the desk.

"I need another appointment for two weeks."

"Earlier the better or you going to arrange for a day off?"

"Probably a day off. I want to get this one done."

"Aren't you always anxious to get it finished," Zerk asked with a chuckle without looking away from the laptop.

"This time it's special." He didn't realize he'd reached across his body to lay his palm over it until the wrap moved under his hand.

Twitch turned to stare at his side. Crave gritted his teeth when he watched Zerk put his arm across Twitch's thighs, and Twitch started ruffling the thick hair on the other man's forearm. His anger must've shown because Twitch instantly dropped his gaze.

What the hell was it with all these men thinking they could touch Twitch all the time? His man should be coming to him.

When have you given him a reason to trust you?

His inner voice called him on his bullshit. He hated that fucking voice. Crave swore he'd killed off his conscience at least a decade ago.

"Midweek would be best, Tank wouldn't mind covering me, and Elijah's rarely on premises during the week."

On the nights Elijah was there, it was all hands on deck. His bosses took the safety of their husband seriously, not that they wouldn't jump in front of Elijah to take a fucking bullet. Elijah was the first to jump to their defense no matter the consequences and the man saved him a time or two over the last few years.

Crave was going to have to straighten his act up. His surly ways weren't going to get his boy. Shit, he was so fucked.

"How about Wednesday at noon?"

"That would work. I'll let them know tonight."

23

He pulled his shirt off his shoulder and pulled it over his head, pushed his arms through the sleeve and—

"Wait, you're about to." Twitch leaned sideways.

Twitch's soft fingertips stroked the skin right above where the tape held the covering in place. He froze at the first contact of Twitch's fingers on his skin. Crave went out of his way to avoid touching Twitch. It had always proved too much temptation.

"You're going to pull the tape off."

His cock jerked at the agonizingly slow touch and then Twitch stared at the distorted image.

"An angel?"

Green eyes peered up at him from beneath long, thick lashes, a bit of liner surrounded the almond shape.

"Something wrong with angels?"

"N-no."

Twitch started to reach for Zerk's arm again, and Crave's hand shot out to catch his wrist. He stroked the quick, building crescendo of Twitch's pulse.

"You going to be home before work?"

"Actually, Twitch has an appointment with me." Trouble stepped up with a smile on his face. "You ready for this?"

"I don't know, it's gonna hurt."

"I'm excellent at my job, Twitch, but would you like someone to hold your hand?"

"I'll go—"

"No," Crave cut Priest off.

Terror darkened Twitch's eyes from dark jade to forest green, and the pupil pushed the iris aside.

"Priest can come with me."

Twitch didn't exactly jerk away, but the man couldn't get away from him fast enough. Everyone seemed to ignore

Crave, but he'd felt the weight of their gazes for a second before the tension in the shop faded.

"You said you wanted privacy, so we'll go in the other room. I'm already set up. Just take off your shirt, and I'll be as quick as I can, promise."

Crave watched the three men disappear into the room marked Private, but before the door closed Twitch lifted his shirt. Scars covered Twitch's stomach and ribs, he made a move to storm around the desk. A strong hand gripped his bicep, and he spun ready to strike.

"Leave it fucking be, it's none of your business," Lucky's voice was cold.

They'd butted heads plenty of times but never came to blows. He'd seen the man in action and knew Lucky wouldn't go down easy.

"Who fucking—"

"I know the blond stunts your thinking process, so I'll repeat, it's none of your business."

Crave jerked away and made his way for the door. Someone had scarred Twitch's perfect, tanned skin, made him fear and there wasn't a damn thing he could do about it. His heart pounded in his chest as his adrenaline spiked, he ripped open the door and disappeared through it. His business or not, he was sure as fuck going to get an answer whether Twitch or the rest of them liked it or not. He was done playing nice, and everyone would learn no one dared touch what was his.

4 SHIT, TWITCH WAS IN TROUBLE

Bodies pushed in three deep around the bar, Twitch and Hunter were running their asses off. Luckily, Hunter wasn't a klutz behind the bar, and they moved smoothly around each other. Sweat rolled down the indent of his spine, and he quickly twisted his hair up into a bun as he took an order.

He pushed opened the cooler and pulled out four bottles, he set them on the rail and quickly popped the tops. That was pretty much the routine for the next hour until they finally started slowing down.

"Hunter, I'm taking fifteen, you got this," Twitch asked.

Hunter nodded, and Twitch quickly ducked beneath the apron. He needed a break from the flirting and the invites to party after he got off work. Twitch moved along the wall until he ducked into the hallway leading to Scary's office and the restrooms. He pushed open the door to the women's room and locked it behind him.

With a heavy sigh, he leaned back against it and closed his eyes. The closed door only muffled the music and didn't do anything to alleviate his growing headache. He raised his hands to curve them around the back of his neck and massage the tight muscles. Tilting his head from side to side he stretched and pushed away from the door. He hurried to relieve himself.

Twitch jumped at the sound of a big body banging into the door, and he was thankful he locked it. He took deep even breaths as he walked to the sink to wash his hands. Peering into the mirror, Twitch studied his face and took in the dark circles his cover up barely concealed. He placed his hands flat on the cold tile.

He felt his control slipping. Only two days had passed since he'd gone to Lucky and Priest's. Although he tried to stick to once a week, he was going to ruin his routine. A schedule was important to lessen his anxiety. Twitch had the next day off, and it was his weekly appointment with his therapist.

"Back to work, Harrison," He told his reflection and headed toward the door, there was another loud bang.

Great, Twitch pulled his phone from his back pocket and opened a message thread with Crave. He unlocked the door quietly and peeked out, he squeaked as the door flew open. He fell back against the wall.

"Well, aren't you fucking pretty," A slurred voice and a rush of alcohol-scented breath fanned his face.

Fear was like a fist around his throat. His vision dimmed at the edges as large hands gripped his hips painfully and pulled him against the man's hard—he closed his eyes tight as he tapped the screen on his phone.

"Now, boy, why don't you show me what that sexy mouth can do," The stranger groaned.

He started to fight the hold the man had on him as a huge hand grabbed his crotch and painfully squeezed him. Twitch kicked and screamed, but a hard mouth slammed down on his. As quickly as it was there is was gone.

Twitch slid down the wall as he tried to push everything away, waiting for the next touch—the next blow. Then he heard a yell filled with agony and the sickening sound of fists connecting with flesh. His eyes flew open to find Crave's wide back blocking his view as Crave repeatedly punched the smaller man beneath him. All hell broke loose as the Brawlers Crew descended, even with their combined efforts they couldn't get Crave off him.

"Crave," his voice barely above a whisper, but Crave instantly stopped and turned to him.

Within seconds he was held in massive arms and tears flowed down his cheeks as he sobbed. Crave's hand cupped his jaw and forced his face up.

"Let me look at you, shit."

Through his tears, he watched Crave grimace and Twitch flinched as Crave's thumb stroked his bottom lip. That's when he registered the taste of blood.

"Motherfucker," Crave growled and started to turn.

Twitch twisted his hands in Crave's shirt and wouldn't let go. The last time Crave had to spend the night in jail there'd been a so-called accident.

He knew the man could easily shake him off, but Crave didn't. Twitch felt exposed as Crave ran his gaze over his face and lower to his body. Outside the little bubble where Crave and he existed, he could hear curses, more blows as the crew took out the trash.

"Come on, baby, let's get some ice on that lip."

He'd never heard Crave's voice that soft and gentle before. Crave quickly stood with Twitch still cradled in his arms. The spectators in the hallway jumped to the sides to let Crave through, and Twitch hid his face against the big man's throat.

His face heated as he found himself set on the bar and Crave took a seat on the stool, positioning himself between his thighs. A first aid kit appeared beside his hip.

"You okay, Twitch." Scary reached up to take his chin and turn his face to the light.

"I'm fine."

"The fuck he," Crave bit off whatever he was going to say. "This is gonna sting."

It was all the warning he'd got before a wet cloth pressed to his lip. He hissed through his clenched teeth. The furrows between Crave's brows deepened, and his mouth tightened into a thin line.

"I'm fine." He tried to sound convincing yet knew it fell flat.

"You're not fine, quit fucking lying. After I get you cleaned up, I'm taking you home."

He didn't bother arguing, he wanted to go home, shower and then sneak out to Lucky and Priest's. The panic was like a small annoying buzz in his head. Ready to build and expand until it tore him apart, but he wouldn't do that there—not in front of Crave.

"Here, honey." Elijah held out his hand with one white pill in the center. "Don't deny you need it."

He carefully took it, placed it on his tongue and took the bottle of water Elijah's handed him.

"Crave's gonna take you home, get you showered and tuck you into bed. We'll call or be by tomorrow to check on you."

Elijah reached up and took his cheeks, tugging him down until he could brush a kiss to his forehead.

"What happened—" Twitch started to ask, but Elijah cut him off.

"Taken care of, that's all you need to know," Elijah's tone didn't invite him to ask for more information.

Elijah released him, and Twitch found himself scooped back into Crave's arms. They were headed for the door when Hunter handed him his bag.

"Your phone is inside."

He barely had time to say thanks before Crave whisked him outside and to his bike. He'd ridden with Bull or Psycho a time or two, but Crave never offered.

"Can you hold on?"

"Yes," he answered as he found himself placed on the back of Crave's bike.

Crave mounted and reached back to tap his thigh. "Scoot up."

Twitch did and then slid his arms through the straps of his backpack. Crave handed him Crave's helmet, and he was about to argue until Crave glared at him until he put it on. So much for Crave staying sweet. He fastened the chin strap and slid in closer to Crave until he could wrap his arms around the big man's waist. It wasn't long until they were speeding toward the farm and then he'd go spend time with Lucky and Priest.

5 CRAVE NEEDED TO CHANNEL THE RAGE

Twitch had tried to sneak away on him. He'd heard the man's soft steps as soon as Twitch crept out of his room. Crave had forbidden the man to leave and took his keys. An hour later, they were still tucked inside his pocket.

The rage was too close to the surface. His crew stole Crave's release from him. He had to channel it somehow, and that's why he was in the barn. The heavy bag swung wildly as he took out his rage on the battle-scarred bag. The sounds of flesh hitting vinyl loud in the night only filled with animals scurrying about outside and in the corners of the building. There was the ring they used to settle arguments.

Unfortunately, no one was around to challenge. Psycho was always up for it. The other man's fuse was as short as his.

Growing up, he'd watched his father take out his anger on anyone or anything in his way. Crave's mother took the brunt of it until Crave got big enough to take the punishment for her. He was too much like his old man. It's one of the reasons he earned his name because he craved violence. At one time, it had been a point of pride being the biggest and baddest. That was until he hired on at Brawlers.

They worked in an environment that fostered an undercurrent of violence waiting to erupt. He landed another combination. It kept their natures under control.

Well, Elijah kept Scary and Tank grounded, it intensified when Juvie their adopted daughter joined the family.

Crave hadn't met a man who instilled a sense of calm, until Twitch. But he didn't have Twitch. The small man had no interest in him.

He caught the bag and pressed his sweaty forehead to it. Crave breathed in deep through his nose, then out through his mouth and repeated. He was tired. He knew everyone thought he was crazy and he went out of his way to prove it.

He was aware that men wanted him. He'd never had an issue, but he was starting to wonder if…he wanted more. He just didn't know if he could have it.

"I made dinner," Twitch's quiet voice came from behind him.

He darted a glance over his shoulder, Twitch was standing just inside the open doors. Twitch's lip was swollen, and he was in his non-work clothes that hung on his thin frame. Crave noticed Twitch wore one of his shirts that hung to his knees. Twitch tended to steal his shirts when he did the laundry. His possessiveness had reached a dangerous level over the last six months or so, and Twitch in his clothes turned him on every fucking time.

Crave pushed aside the thoughts and tried to think of safer subjects. Crave had always wanted to ask what it was about housework and cooking that the man liked so much. Saturday mornings he cleaned the house, he assigned each of them a laundry day. Crave's fell on the same day Twitch did his. Menus for the week were tacked up every Sunday. They swore the house would fall apart if it weren't for Twitch running it.

"A little early, the guys won't be home for another hour or two. I needed something to do. I already made them plates and set them in the oven."

"Let me grab a shower, and we can eat."

"Okay." Twitch started to pivot on his toes.

"Twitch?"

"Yeah?"

"You okay?"

"I just needed—"

"Something to do, that's not what I asked."

"I'll be okay. As long as I'm busy, I'm all right."

"Give me about twenty."

"I'll set the table."

"Thanks."

Twitch's eyes widened at him saying thanks and Crave grimaced. He was such an asshole.

"You're welcome."

Twitch escaped quickly and Crave followed at a slower pace as he unwrapped his hands. He flexed the stiff muscles and tendons as he strode across the yard, then into the house. He forced himself to continue to his room to grab a towel and a pair of sweats.

Crave walked across the hall to the bathroom. He didn't close the door all the way as he threw his towel and sweats across the back of the toilet. He listened to Twitch move around the kitchen, plates being set on the table and the fridge door opening and closing. He tracked Twitch's movements until he pushed the curtain aside and turned the taps.

He quickly stripped his boots and clothes then stepped under the scalding hot spray. Crave turned and tipped his head back to wet his hair. That's when he caught Twitch's scent. It was clean, mint and citrus. He inhaled it deep into his lungs as he stroked his hands down his hairy chest and stomach. The deep ridges of his abdomen tightened as he fisted his cock in his right hand. Twitch's scent, the sight of his long hair down his back, hell, anything about Twitch caused his dick to harden.

He pumped his cock picturing Twitch. His tight, high, little ass. Fuck, he wanted his hand print on it. He widened his stance as he rolled his balls in his left hand and tugged. Jerking off was an empty release, but he needed it. A little something just to take the edge off before he had to sit across the table from Twitch and not be allowed to touch.

Crave started a quick, brutal rhythm as he shifted his feet as far apart as the tub allowed. Biting back his groans as his balls ached and his dick jerked in his grip. He pictured Twitch's face, imagined what he'd look like naked and kneeling before him. As an image formed in his head of marking Twitch's tanned skin with his seed, he lost it. He pulled at his shaft lengthening his pleasure as he looked down to see his hand covered with his release. The last beads of cum dripping from the fat head.

Every muscle in his body was seized up as the remnants of pleasure moved over his body as he jerked. He placed his hands on the wall and leaned forward as he drew in deep breaths. The ecstasy fled, disappointment in its wake, and he turned to efficiently clean up. Crave wanted more. He needed Twitch in his bed. He craved the right to claim Twitch for everyone to see and know Twitch belonged only to him.

He quickly turned off the water and stepped over the side of the tub. He dried his body in rough strokes then pulled on his sweats. Crave hung his towel on the rack on the back of the door and pulled it open to head to the kitchen. He finger-combed his hair.

Twitch was just setting a beer in front of the plate that had to be his. It overflowed with food, and Twitch didn't drink. Twitch couldn't drink with the meds he took. There was so much about Twitch he was curious about, but never asked.

"Bull texted and said they'd be home in an hour or so."

"Rough night?"

"No, they cleared everyone out not long after we left. They're just hanging out for a bit. Sit, food's going to get cold."

Crave took his seat and Twitch sat in the spot across from him. "Looks great." Crave stared down at his plate. It was his favorite. Some Italian casserole loaded with cheese and meat, a loaf of Twitch's homemade bread was sliced and arranged on a plate between them.

"Why do you like to cook so much and take care of the house?"

"It's busy work and also y'all don't do it right."

"The truth, Twitch."

"I like to cook and clean, but Bull let me move in without question when he found out I had nowhere to go. I don't think he asks enough in rent, so I do what I can."

"Why did you leave college?"

"My parents stopped paying my tuition. They decided to come for a surprise visit, and I wasn't alone in the apartment they rented for me."

"Boyfriend?"

Twitch laughed. "No, he was my best friend and because everything was paid and he didn't have a lot." Twitch shrugged. "I let him stay. We were just curled up to watch a movie."

"And your parents flipped over that?"

"They're fanatical about propriety and image."

"So you're supposed to be a virgin with you married the perfect woman?"

"No, just as long as I was a virgin they didn't care whether it was a man or woman. It's not like a look very butch, Crave." Twitch gave a cute little roll of his eyes.

"True."

"Thanks," Twitch muttered sarcastically.

"You're welcome."

"Eat." Twitch pointed to Crave's plate with his fork.

"Fine," Crave muttered and started eating, he remained silent until he was halfway through. He'd watched Twitch the entire time, Twitch ate all proper with one no elbows on the table. Twitch took delicate bites. Crave wondered if that's the way Twitch grew up. "You've never visited your parents."

"I visit, but it's uncomfortable."

"Why?"

"Because I'm a bartender in a gay biker bar and I live in a houseful of single men. According to them, I'm probably a whore."

"Bullshit, I can't remember the last time—"

A thought hit him. Other than Twitch sneaking out, he'd never seen the man go home with anyone or even date. Did that mean—no, a man like Twitch wasn't untouched.

"Because I've never. Sex is bad. It's for procreation only. But in my case when I married it would be to a woman, and sex a duty."

"Are your parents insane? Fucking isn't bad and should never be a duty."

"I wouldn't know, so can we change the subject?"

"But where do you go when you sneak out?"

"Priest and Lucky let me…they ground me and make me feel safe. It has nothing to do with sex."

"You don't feel—"

"Can we just eat?"

Twitch had a bit of a temper himself because he gave his plate a death glare and angrily moved his food around it.

"They were actually trying to marry me off."

"Arranged marriage," He joked, but the heat infusing Twitch's cheeks caused him to drop his fork. When it clanged against the plate Twitch jumped from his chair. "Twitch, do you think I'd—"

The thought Twitch would think he'd put his hands on him in anger grated at Crave's insecurities and fears.

"I have to get the dishes done and get to bed, I have an appointment in the morning. I'm going to need my keys."

"They're in my jeans."

"Did you leave your clothes on the floor again?"

"No," Crave lied.

"Dammit, I've told you so many times not to leave your clothes lying around," Twitch's voice faded as he disappeared.

He laughed at the man's bitching. It was like they were already married. Crave jumped from his chair and jogged toward the bathroom in time to catch Twitch angrily picking Crave's clothes off the floor.

"The floor is wet. Did your parents not teach you," the man let out a frustrated scream.

Twitch reached around him to drag Crave's towel off the back of the door to mop up the small amount of water on the floor.

"What am I going to do with you?"

A highly inappropriate answer tripped and stopped on the tip of his tongue. His plan would involve them in bed for days until Twitch swore he was his. Crave leaned his shoulder against the wall and just watched Twitch as he mumbled and straightened the mess Crave made. For him it was a done deal, Twitch was going to have his ring on his finger, but Twitch just didn't know it yet.

6 DAMMIT, HE WASN'T A KID!

His fingers gripped the sides of the pillow until his knuckles went white. A satisfying image of smothering Crave brought a smile to his face. The man wouldn't leave. Everywhere he turned lately there he was, at work, and even at home. He hadn't gone to Lucky and Priest's for almost two weeks, and his anxiety grew worse. It was one night, he was completely selfish, and Crave was taking that away from him.

"He's not worth the jail time."

He turned his head to find Bull filling the doorway. The sexy, silver fox crossed his arms over his chest and raised a thick salt and pepper brow.

"I'm debating that."

"Twitch, you've known Crave four years, and in all that time he hasn't changed. You got hurt on his watch, and you know what that means."

"He's going to stalk me for the rest of my life."

Bull chuckled. "Probably."

"You're so fucking encouraging."

"Come here." Bull held out his arms and Twitch quickly walked into them.

He nuzzled the thick hair under his cheek and hugged Bull's waist tight. As short as he was, he only reached Bull's sternum. It wasn't the same as when he got to snuggle between his two best friends, but it was close. That edge of anxiety he lived with receded a bit.

Bull kissed the top of his head and then turned to rest of cheek on the spot he'd just kissed.

"Twitch, you knew when you got the job at Brawlers that we were going to be highly protective."

"I know that, and I appreciate it, I do, but he won't even let me out of the house."

"You do know where the keys to my truck are."

Twitch sighed. "If it was only that easy. It's like he senses when I leave my room."

"He's great at his job for a reason, and he's the most observant man I've ever met. Have you tried talking to him?"

He knew that. Crave was Second to Head of Security because he was excellent at his job. He loved all the guys, but he felt safer when Crave worked the door. Twitch didn't want to think about it too much. It always came back to the fact he'd instantly found Crave attractive, even harbored a stupid crush since he'd started working at Brawlers. That would definitely never go anywhere.

"Oh that works, he doesn't care about anyone's opinion but his own."

"Quit being bitchy. If Crave understood maybe he'd relax."

"I don't want to tell him." To put all his shit out there, expose all his fucked up thoughts, and prove just how crazy he was. He'd confessed enough when they'd had dinner.

"The way you grew up wasn't your fault."

He pulled back to tilt his chin up to look at Bull's concerned expression.

"I know that I know it wasn't normal. Sex isn't bad. I shouldn't feel the need to punish—"

"I thought we'd discussed this."

"I haven't cut in months." The response became automatic. He hated to make his friends worry about him. Twitch loved them, but it became annoying. Just another reminder he wasn't normal.

"Have you tried—"

"Masturbation isn't the answer, and it only freaks me out."

"It's your dick. It was put there for more reasons than pissing."

Twitch rolled his eyes. "Fuck, you're so eloquent."

"I try."

"It just makes me anxious."

"Jerking off is supposed to be—"

"Why the fuck are you talking to him about jerking off," Crave's pissed off voice broke them apart. "And why the fuck are you touching him?"

"Fuck you, man, I can hold him as much as I want."

Bull tightened his hold and Twitch knew the older man only did it to piss Crave off more. For all Bull's position as a father-figure, the man was as much or bigger asshole than all of them.

"The fuck you can."

This wasn't going to end well. The last time Bull and Crave went several rounds in the ring, he'd had a bitch of a time stitching them up.

"Hey, he is standing right here. Shit, you two are impossible." He hurried back to Crave's bed and finished making it. The whole time he could feel Crave staring at him. Twitch knew if he turned around he'd find Crave's fists clenched at his sides. The man was continuously battle-ready.

He bent and gathered up the pile of linens. Twitch turned to find Bull gone, but Crave blocking the door.

"Why do you have to touch everybody?"

"What are you talking about?"

"You touch everyone, and they seemed to think they have the right to touch you."

"It's comforting. Touching doesn't equal sex."

Crave placed his hands on his lean hips and dropped his chin to his chest. Twitch noticed he was doing that breathing thing Crave did when he was about to lose his temper. He didn't doubt Crave would never hurt him. The man always protected him even if he bitched at him afterward. Crave never touched him at all. The day at Twirled was the first time in four years he'd ever felt the man's hands. The night of the attack was the second.

He'd never noticed before that Crave went out of his way to not touch him. The realization hurt, and he didn't know why. Shit, he knew why. Twitch just didn't want to admit it to himself.

"Why are you doing your relaxation breathing?"

"Give me a minute," Crave barked out.

Twitch rolled his lips between his teeth to suppress a smile. The man's crankiness amused him some days.

"Are you smiling?"

"Of course not." He ruined it by feeling the corners of his mouth tug into a smile.

"Liar. Today is not my scheduled day for room cleaning."

"I woke Hunter up and he told me to go away, Psycho locks his room except on his day. Why you asking?"

"No reason."

"I used gloves to move your lube to your nightstand and to remove your sheets. I've seen where you've been. You're also low, should I put it on the grocery list?"

"Funny man."

Crave hadn't brought anyone home in a while. Crave was fond of screamers, so his lack of bed partners was noticeable. Living in a house full of healthy, highly sexual men, he'd learned to invest in several pairs of ear buds. Loud and abrasive music was his friend on those nights.

"Today is our laundry day, though."

"Bossy, I'll grab the basket and take it to—"

"Got it." He dropped the sheets on top of Crave's basket.

"I'll carry it downstairs."

Crave picked up the basket and took it from the room. Twitch followed close behind. He'd already taken his own laundry to the basement. It was just a matter of separating Crave's clothes into the piles he'd already made. And, yes, he'd swipe a shirt like he always did, just one, but he was getting a pretty good collection. They were the perfect size for sleeping in, and that was the only thing he'd admit to because the truth was embarrassing.

The big man never mentioned it even though he had to be missing the shirts. Crave jogged down the steps, but Twitch took them at a slower pace. The basement was finished, but was empty except for some boxes and the washer and dryer, with a table for folding.

"Oh, I'm going out later."

"Where?"

"Elijah, Brody and I are going to dinner. Tank, Scary and Trouble are going to watch the kids. I might not be–"

"You'll be home. I don't want you out all night."

"I'm not a fucking kid, Crave. I'm a grown man, and I can come and go as I please. You can't tell me what to do." Fuck, didn't that make him sound like the kid he was being treated like?

"You'll do as I—"

"Fuck you and do your own laundry." He ran back up the steps, grabbed his backpack and keys and headed out the door with Crave yelling his name.

"I'm done with you and your attitude. I've had enough."

"Twitch, I'm not going to argue with you. Get the fuck back in the house."

Crave barreled toward him, his face red with anger, but Twitch still wasn't scared—he was mad.

"No, I'm twenty-five, not five. You're not the boss of me."

"Now you're not sounding like you're five at all."

"Crave, stand down," Bull bellowed as he stepped between them. "Twitch, get in the car and go."

Twitch opened his door, got in and slammed it behind him. Crave tried to get around Bull, and that's when all hell broke loose. Psycho came running from the house. It was the last thing he saw as he spun tires as he drove toward the main road. Instead of heading for town, he turned in the opposite direction. He needed some time alone. He'd text Brody and Elijah later. Right now he just wanted to disappear, and he knew just the place to go.

7 TWITCH DIDN'T FUCKING COME HOME

Motherfucker, he pounded the heavy bag with brutal punches and kicks. Sweat dampened his hair and body, he hadn't slept all night waiting for Twitch to come home. He'd searched for him everywhere, even went to Lucky and Priest's place. Priest had told him to fuck off and slammed the door in his face.

Crave apparently was on everyone's shit list, especially Bull's. He didn't hear but sensed someone behind him. He just kept trying to work out his anger. What the hell did he think he was going to do with Twitch? Crave was just like his father filled with rage. He didn't deserve Twitch.

"Done being an asshole," Landon angrily asked from behind him.

"Isn't that standard M.O. for me?"

"Quit acting stupid."

Ah yes, Brody too, could his fucking day get any worse? Not only was he sporting several stitches, a black eye and a busted lip he now had to deal with Twitch's best friends.

"What do y'all want?"

"We want to know why Twitch is in hiding?"

Landon kept his distance, but he knew the man could be vicious when required. Scary taught Landon everything he knew. Which made Landon extremely dangerous.

"I didn't do—"

"You did, Twitch won't even answer his phone and barely answers our texts." Brody tried to pull off looking intimidating.

The cute guy wasn't badass in the least.

"What the fuck do y'all want from me?"

"To quit being a bastard. No matter what you think you're not dear old dad."

"You don't know—"

He growled at Landon's habit of cutting people off when he doesn't want to hear what they say.

"Twitch has enough issues of his own. He doesn't need you adding yours."

"Then what the hell am I supposed to do?"

"Twitch has been taught sex is bad. Arousal is a sin."

His mind brought up the mental picture of Twitch's scars. The ones he'd thought someone else put there.

"How long?"

"How long what?"

Landon was playing stupid with him, and Brody looked everywhere but at him. How many knew and never told him? Elijah knew Twitch needed a pill after the attack. Bull was talking to Twitch about masturbation. Twitch told him a bit about his past, but not a lot.

"You know what, how long has he been cutting himself?"

"If you want to know anything you'll ask him."

The man needed to stop busting his balls.

"He's not exactly talking to me."

"That's your own fault. So what are you doing to do about it," Landon asked.

"There's nothing I can do." Crave raised his hands and roughly shoved his fingers through his hair.

"Yes, there is. Call him or have an actual conversation with him where you aren't acting like you're his father."

"None of my feelings toward Twitch are fatherly."

"Then, Crave, why did you tell him he couldn't stay out all night. Ordered him home." Brody took a step away from the doorway.

"After the other night, he didn't need to be out alone."

Crave noticed neither man moved toward him. They stayed near the door, and as he walked closer, he saw Trouble, Bull, and Zerk just outside. Did his friends think he'd hurt Brody and Landon? That hurt more than he'd expected, so he retreated to stand next to the bag.

"I'd never put my hands on your men."

Bull stepped inside. "Crave." The man sighed, "You've been out of control for months now. You're a Brawler. No damn way are you backing down from a battle, but you sure as fuck are causing more—"

"Is this an intervention?"

"Maybe, but it's necessary. Both you and Twitch live here, you drove Twitch from his home, and I can't have that shit. Either you fucking straighten up, or you can leave. This is the only warning I'm giving. Fix this mess you made."

Everyone left without another word, and he stumbled back to take a seat on a bench against a far wall. He buried his face in his hands. Crave was going to lose his home. The one place in his life he didn't feel like running from, and he knew Bull didn't make idle threats. He should go ahead and pack his shit because he'd fucked up.

He wearily pushed to his feet, jerked his shirt from the bench and quickly strode outside and then across the yard. Once he was inside with a locked door between him and everyone else he sat on the edge of his bed. He picked his phone up from the nightstand.

Crave stroked his thumb across the screen and went to his messages. The last one he had from Twitch was from the other night. Nothing but gibberish. He held his phone in both hands, and his thumbs hovered over the keyboard.

What the hell was he going to say? Would he accept sorry?

He tossed the phone on his pillow and fell back on the bed.

"Quit being a chicken shit."

Psycho's voice had him curling up and found the man leaned back against the closet door.

"What the fuck are you doing here? You're not going to start too, are ya?"

There was one person he didn't want to take on, and that was Psycho. The man wasn't exactly right. The first time he'd met Psycho he'd walked up to the guy who'd kidnapped Elijah until Ian's gun was pressed to the center of his chest. Psycho had dared Ian to shoot him as he had a relaxed conversation with Elijah. Someone like that you didn't fuck with too much.

"I'm just here to make sure you don't fuck up my calm."

"Calm, when have you ever been calm?"

"Since I've been here and I like it as is, so I'm going to help you fix it."

Psycho was the last one who'd be considered empathetic. He was crazier than Crave, and that was saying a lot.

"And how are you going to do that?"

"You're just fucking full of questions."

"I've got no clue what I'm doing."

"That's truth. Twitch is all delicate and shit, but he puts on a good front. That boy got one helluva poker face. But if Scary and Tank got a man like Elijah—"

"You're obsessed with their boy. You know they ain't sharing, right?"

"I don't want Elijah, I just want one like him. If I can figure out how the fuck they did it."

"Like I said obsessed."

"So are you, with Twitch and quit trying to change the subject. Pick up the damn phone and tell him you're sorry."

He reached back and wrapped his hand around his phone. "What if he doesn't accept it?"

"Either you try, or you're packing your shit."

"If I knew where he was. I could do this in person."

"Not happening, they know where he is, but no address and not the full name of his friend."

"He's with—"

"No, don't start your bullshit. Call him or text him, fucking do it. Also, I'm hungry, and Twitch didn't leave leftovers."

"Go into town or make your own—"

"I'm not dying from food poisoning, and tonight he was making my favorite, I can't get that in town. No one makes Empanadas like he does. I might see about getting himself just for the food."

"Get the fuck out," Crave bellowed.

He barely caught the micro smile, but it was there. That fucker was playing him. Psycho unlocked the door and left him alone. They were all getting on his nerves. Instead of a text, he tried calling. Part of him knew Twitch wasn't going to answer, but that was okay. It would probably be easier if he didn't.

Crave listened to the rings, and finally, Twitch's voice mail picked up.

"Twitch, I'm a bastard, and I want to explain but, fuck, I can't do that this way. Call me or just come home...please. I'm sorry." He disconnected the call and set the phone back on his nightstand.

He'd never told anyone the full story about his parents. He didn't want to tell Twitch because he'd have to admit to the man that he was just like his father. It was his worst fear that one day the man he'd make his would end up just like his mother. It was the thing that kept him away from Twitch, but he couldn't do it anymore, and he also wasn't willing to have Twitch lose his home. If he could do one thing right, at least he could do that.

It didn't matter one way or another if Twitch didn't come home. Bull would kick his ass and then help him pack his shit. Crave went to take a shower and hoped Twitch came back or at the very least called. He'd fucked up, and he wanted to fix it, but first Twitch had to give him a chance Crave didn't think he deserved.

8 YOU'RE GOING TO CALL CRAVE, RIGHT?

Twitch curled up in the corner of his oldest friend's couch wrapped in a blanket and read the same page of his book for the fifth time. He was halfway through and didn't know what the hell he was reading. Drake and his husband, Paul, were snuggled on the opposite couch. He could feel them staring, and it was starting to make his skin crawl.

He hadn't had friends before Drake. He'd met him the first day of registration his freshman year. Drake hadn't had a family, and it wasn't long after they had met he'd found out Drake slept in his car. Twitch hadn't hesitated to give Drake a place to stay. It had been that way for three years until the day his parents showed up and fucked up his life. Although it wasn't like they hadn't done it before then.

Something that could've been normal, sex had been turned into some punishable sin. Masturbation was something to cause shame. He couldn't even look at his body anymore without focusing on the scars. The pain he'd used to push away his desire.

Crave made him want to change. Caused him to feel things he knew he shouldn't. He'd listened to Crave's message a dozen times. Crave said he was sorry and wanted to explain but explain what?

Drake broke the silence first, "You're going to call him, right?"

He didn't even pretend not to know who the *he* Drake spoke of was and decided not to answer at all.

"Evan, don't be an ass."

He grimaced at the use of his real name. It had been so long since anyone used it and since he'd been appointed Twitch, he liked it more.

"He treated me like a kid."

"We know that, but are you going to keep pretending you don't love the man. Please, every conversation we've had for the last few years is Crave this and Crave that."

"I don't love him."

"Yes, you do," Paul said with a snort.

"Four years ago, you pretty much disappeared off the face of the earth for a year. Then when I do hear from you, what do I find out?" Drake paused. "Oh yes, you're living in communal housing with a bunch of bar bouncers and bikers, and working as a bartender."

"There's nothing wrong with my job."

"I didn't say there was. You wanted a different life, and that's what you got, but you're still—"

"If you say I'm still living in the past I'm going to leave."

"You're not going anywhere. What you're going to do is go to your room and call Crave. You're an adult, and you're going to act like one."

"Not you too," Twitch whined and threw himself down on the couch, pulling a tantrum worthy of a professional two-year-old.

He heard Drake and Paul laughing, he turned his head and stared at them.

"Why do y'all hate me?"

"We don't hate you, we love you, but you're due back at work tomorrow. And I don't think your cute, pink loungewear is exactly going to work."

"I can go home after I know he's—"

"No, Twitch." Drake pushed up from the couch and walked around the coffee table.

Twitch watched his friend grab Twitch's phone off the table.

"What are you doing?"

"What you should be doing." Drake started scrolling through the contacts.

Twitch jumped from the couch, but his taller friend held him back pressing the phone to his ear.

"Don't do that, dammit, Drake, I'll never—"

"Twitch," Crave's voice could be heard clearly, "Baby, you there?"

The question came through the speaker as Drake held the phone up and away.

"Is this Crave?"

"Who the fuck are you and where's my boy?"

He said he hated it, that he'd never be Crave's submissive, even if Crave claimed not to be a dominant. The man had all the characteristics except for control. That was one thing Crave didn't possess. Twitch loved the *my* and *mine* thing Crave had going on.

"Boy, sounds kinky."

Twitch groaned and fell back on the couch. That was going to open up a whole new line of questioning.

"Something you want to tell me, Evan?"

Twitch shook his head until he made himself dizzy.

"Evan, who the fuck is Evan," Crave yelled louder.

"Twitch never told you his real name?"

"Evan, I don't like it, where's Twitch?"

"My best friend is currently laying on the couch giving me a death glare."

Drake had way too much fun with this shit. Why had he ever called the man his best friend?

"And why aren't you home?"

And we were back to why aren't you home.

"I'm not a kid, Crave."

"I'm aware of that. Could we have this conversation without an audience? Please."

"He said please, you can't tell him no. Go to your room—"

"His room is here. His home is here, where he should be."

Twitch surged to his feet and grabbed the phone, he took off at a run to lock himself in the guest room.

"Twitch, Twitch, are you there?"

"Hold on, I'm locking the door," he said as he took the phone off speaker. Twitch didn't trust Paul and Drake not to press their ears to the door to listen in.

"Are you safe, tell me where you are so I can come and get you."

"I'm fine, Drake and his husband are crazy, but I'm safe."

"Did you get my message?"

"Yes."

"Then why didn't you call?"

Crave almost sounded sad, and Twitch didn't know how to handle that. The big blond was happy and angry, sometimes pouting, but never sad.

"I didn't know what to say."

"Easy, you didn't come home, and I was worried. You've never stayed away from home overnight."

"You have to stop treating me like a kid. I'm an adult. I take care of myself."

"I don't want to do this over the phone."

"Do what?"

"Explain. Shit, I never wanted to tell you."

"Well, this is what you got, so explain."

He heard a heavy sigh and then loud music and voices.

"You're at work, not a place to be distracted."

"I just told Tank I needed a few, let me walk around the side."

The creak of the wooden bench came through and a minute of silence. He almost thought Crave changed his mind until he heard the man clear his throat.

"I'm just like my dad, angry, but I'm not a drunk like him. For as long as I can remember he took all his shit out on everyone. My mom. Me. I got real good at taking a punch early."

He said Crave's name, but Crave continued.

"Mom just kept taking it. My hometown was a shit hole, probably still is. All the people were hollow-eyed and broken, especially the women. The kids, we did whatever to escape, drinking, drugs, or sex, a combo of all."

"What happened to your mom?"

"Too many years of beatings, the docs say trauma brought on early dementia. I pay for Nettie to stay in a nice facility."

"Is that where you go almost every Sunday?"

"Yeah, but she doesn't know who I am all the time. It's been about four years since she said my name. One thing every small town has is sports. I swore to her when I scored a football scholarship I wouldn't be him and I'd never come back. She made me promise."

"I'm sorry." Twitch's heart broke at the misery evident in Crave's voice. He was wishing he went home for their conversation. Crave didn't touch him, but Twitch wanted to hug him.

"Nothing to be sorry for, my childhood was better than some, maybe worse than others. We all got our shit."

He didn't like the way the man shrugged it off when Twitch knew it had to hurt on some level. Just like his past molded him, Crave's did the same to him.

"What does this—"

"I swore never to be him. I fuck the temporary ones because I'm sure I'm going to fuck up a man's life."

"How do you know that?"

"Twitch, you've known me for years now."

"Yeah, you're an asshole, abrasive, and quick to start or as you say finish a fight. No different than the rest of the Brawlers Crew. Actually, Psycho is worse than you are."

"I'm terrified I'll hurt my man."

"You think you'd—"

"I am my old—"

"No, you're not him. You've always taken care of me. Protected me, I know it's your job, but you've never hesitated, don't you think you'd do that for…a boyfriend or partner?"

Twitch always knew he was too fucked up to get past his hang-ups, and the whole virgin thing wasn't Crave's type, but he hated the thought of Crave with other men.

He'd probably ruined his hearing with loud music all the nights Crave brought someone home.

"I don't think I know how. When are you coming back?"

That was Crave's signal he was done, but Twitch knew Crave needed to get back to work. Most of the time working the door was a two-man job.

"I'll be home tomorrow. I just need time."

"You've had time."

"I've only been gone a day."

"A day too long. Also, Psycho threatened me because last night was his Empanadas."

"Oh shit, I screwed up his routine. He hates change. Is he okay?"

"The bastard is good. He can do without—"

"No, the routine makes it easier for him to function. Change makes him anxious."

"Is that why you have all your plans and schedules, the housework and cooking?"

"Yeah," Twitched answered.

"I saw the scars."

"How? I'm careful," Twitch heard his voice break.

He'd always been vigilant about making sure he was clothed all the time, even at night in case of emergencies. His eyes started to burn knowing Crave saw what he'd only shown a few people.

"The day Trouble took you in the back room. You lifted your shirt before the door closed. Why?"

"Easy answer, the pain lets me feel. Years of suppressing any sensation that was even the least bit enjoyable. The pain is safe. Anything to do with sex or pleasure...I don't know how to handle it."

"So you cut, are you—"

"It's been several months. Where the pain grounded me before, gave me focus, Lucky and Priest gave me something else."

"I don't—"

"It had nothing to do with sex."

"Still, why didn't you come to Bull, Psycho, or even me?"

"Everyone helps in their own way. It may seem pathetic to you, but the Twirled and Brawlers crews are like security blankets."

"Like when you touch everyone."

"Yes."

"Make me a promise."

"What?"

"When you don't feel grounded or when you feel lost, come to me."

"I don't—"

"Please, you need someone to ground you, and I need someone who won't make me feel like a monster waiting to explode."

"So, we'd help each other?"

Twitch didn't know if he could do it. The thought of putting himself into such close contact with the man he'd come to love over the years terrified him. What happened if Twitch's neediness caused Crave to hate him or find him disgusting, he'd be destroyed.

"Exactly, at least try."

"Okay, you better get back to work. Tank's probably looking for you."

"Yeah, so, I'll see you at work?"

"Probably at the house, I gotta go home and get dressed. I don't think hot pink pajamas with rainbows on them are exactly Brawler attire."

"Really, hot pink?"

"There's nothing wrong with pink."

"Didn't say there was, you own a lot of pink, but hot—"

"Yeah, yeah, quit harping on it. Go back to work."

"Good night, Twitch."

"You too, Crave."

He hesitated to disconnect the call. Twitch hadn't realized until he had heard Crave's voice how much he'd missed him. Communal housing didn't give you much space or privacy, so you were with people day in and day out when you lived and worked with them. He knew everyone's schedule as well as his own.

He fell back onto the bed and stared up at the ceiling, watching the fan blades as they blurred. Since he saw Crave in a new light, not just an arrogant and gorgeous man with moments of over protectiveness he tried to get his brain around it. Twitch never heard Crave admit to being scared or show much weakness at all. To discover just how vulnerable Crave was, shifted his perception of the man.

A momentary urge to get in his car and go home early hit him, but it was too late for the two-hour drive. It definitely wasn't safe and Crave would be pissed if Twitch tried it. He curled upward and stood, and he went to make himself tea and talk with his friends. He needed a sounding board, and he knew he'd get an honest opinion from Drake and Paul, he just hoped like fuck he liked what they said.

9 THIS IS HARDER THAN CRAVE THOUGHT

He was about to rip the fucker's head off, the Executioners were playing Brawlers tonight. The lead singer King plastered himself to Twitch when the big bastard wasn't on stage. King was smooth and charming, a goddamned sweetheart. Except for the whole player thing, the other man would be perfect for Twitch.

That wasn't fucking happening. Crave was trying to keep his cool. Attempting to be the new and approved Crave sucked ass and not in a good fucking way.

The only highlight was Twitch would signal last call at any time. He was tired. Crave hadn't slept with Twitch away from the house.

"The man is relentless, Twitch ain't giving up that ass to anyone especially King."

He turned to find Hunter taking a drag off his e-cig and watching Twitch and King the same as he was.

"He's about to get his fingers broken if he touches Twitch one more time."

"Dude, you gotta relax. Twitch ain't like that. You know how many offers he turns down a night?"

Crave didn't need a reminder. He knew exactly how many. Crave made sure no one ever got his man passed the nearest exit. That wasn't going to change anytime soon.

"You've been acting weird lately, you need to get laid or something."

"Ain't you just talkative as fuck tonight."

"And you're a bigger asshole than normal."

Shit, he was, he was supposed to show Twitch he was good boyfriend material. Kicking King's ass wouldn't do that. He grunted and ducked out the front door, he hoped the out of sight out of mind philosophy would work. Crave had his doubts.

Tank grunted to get his attention, and he turned to look at his boss and friend. The man raised a brow.

"I'm good."

His lips stretched into a smile as Tank signed telling him he was a liar.

"King is flirting with Twitch as usual and don't even say it. I already know Twitch ain't going home with anyone. Doesn't fucking mean I gotta like it."

Tank shrugged his broad shoulders.

"Do y'all live to fuck with me," Crave asked.

Tank nodded his head and slapped his back before heading inside. How the Tank kept two partners happy was beyond him. Scary, Elijah and Tank were perfect together, they each complimented the other. It was the same with all his friends at Twirled. They fought like hell, but in the end, they were just fucking happy.

It was his fault Twitch only saw him as an asshole. His personality was genetic. He didn't know how or if he could change to make Twitch happy. None of his other friends had, and they'd gotten boyfriends and husbands. Some had beautiful little families with kids. He loved his nieces, but he was sure as fuck he couldn't do it. He loved spoiling them and sending them home.

"Asshole," Lucky's annoyed voice came from his left.

"Looks who's talking."

"I'm the one with a hot ass husband, and you're still in the friend zone."

"Fucker," Crave snarled. "Speaking of husbands, where's yours? Finally get tired of your ass, huh?"

"Nope, just came to check on Twitch before I go home. We're putting together nursery furniture tonight."

"How much longer?"

"Twelve weeks. Also, Lou wants Twitch there."

"Why?"

"Because he's pretty much been through every fucking step."

"Really?"

"Yeah, he went with us when they did all that IVF shit and implanted. Lou figured he should be there when she pushes out the parasite."

"Isn't it weird to consider your kid a parasite?"

"Not really, it's what it is, it feeds off its host for ten months."

"Only you, better get in there King is probably talking Twitch into running off with him."

"Doubt it. Twitch is forbidden. No one fucks with him. King also likes huge fuckers like himself, ya know, Bear on Bear action."

He didn't think he believed that. King was on a mission every night the Executioners played Brawlers.

"I better get inside. Priest is expecting me home."

"I gotta make the rounds so if I don't see ya have a good one." Crave nodded as Lucky started passed him. "Hey, man, you get Priest shit all the time."

"My Pretty Bear likes surprises, why?"

"What kinds of things does Twitch like?"

"Oh, well, Twitch is kinda difficult."

"Why?"

"He's not big on material things. Likes snuggling. Coffee. Chocolate."

"Not really helpful."

"I'm a fucking wealth of information. He loves Cyclops and Plague, the rat especially, but I'd talk to him about giving him a living present first."

"Thanks, man."

"Anytime, Priest and me kinda adopted Twitch. If you ain't serious about something permanent, find someone else to fuck with."

It was all Lucky had said before he disappeared inside.

Why did everyone think he only wanted to fuck? The guys gave him shit about Twitch, and that was their way, but it wasn't a joke. He'd put it off for a long time. Crave didn't give a shit what people thought of him, but he did care what Twitch thought.

Crave stood as people started filing out the front exit. Most of them left with someone under their arm or wrapped around them. Slowly the parking lot cleared out except for the crew's vehicles and the band's van. He retook his seat and leaned back against the wall.

"Drink this," Twitch's ordered. "You look like shit."

He took the large mug and inhaled the strong aroma. "Thanks, you're as beautiful as always." And Twitch was.

Twitch always started the night off with his hair down, and by the end, he had it twisted into a loose bun. His big, almond shaped eyes were perfectly lined in black. Twitch's kissable lips shone with a hint of gloss. The man always kept the little makeup he did wear subtle.

"Drink your coffee, you're delirious."

"Take a fucking compliment."

"Quit being an asshole."

"Sorry," Crave mumbled and lifted the mug to his mouth.

"I'm sleepy and cranky," Twitched muttered and leaned into Crave's side.

The action almost caused Crave to wrap his arm around Twitch to pull him closer. He didn't though because he still didn't know if Twitch would run. Crave always resisted touching Twitch. It was too much temptation for him.

"This is where the fuck you're hiding?" Lucky bounded out the door.

"I'm not hiding, plain sight and all that shit."

"Quit being a shit, but what can I expect with the company you're keeping?"

"Don't start, I'm sleepy."

An evil grin pulled at Lucky's lips, and it caused Crave to growl. It was a mistake because he'd given the bastard what he'd wanted. A pointy elbow jabbed him in the ribs and Crave looked down to find Twitch shaking his head.

"You coming over tonight."

"No, I'm going home to my own bed. I crashed at Drake's place the last few nights. They're worse than the Brawlers when it comes to volume."

"Okay, but Lou wants to make sure you're gonna be there for delivery."

"She wants me there?"

"Of course, quit being an idiot. There wasn't any other place you'd be. Besides we thought Evan would be a kick ass middle name."

Twitch didn't make a sound when he launched himself at Lucky. Lucky wrapped Twitch up in his arms.

Crave watched Twitch shake and realized Twitch silently sobbed. He met Lucky's gaze as the man soothingly stroked his hands up and down Twitch's slim back. Where there was usually anger or evil only existed an emotion that looked a lot like what he'd assume love would look like.

What little he knew of Twitch's past didn't seem happy. Fuck, the man had issues with sex, a virgin for fuck's sake. What did he know about being someone's first? And he planned to be that and Twitch's only. Crave never thought he'd find the man who was it for him.

Twitch pulled back from Lucky and scrubbed his hands over his face. Even if they were happy tears, he hated the thought of Twitch crying. What he hated more was the fact Lucky made him happy and Crave only scared or pissed Twitch off.

They'd made a deal, Twitch would come to him from now on when he needed to feel safe and grounded. How the hell was someone like Crave going to do that? He lived with constant chaos and barely controlled rage. Crave wasn't the man for Twitch, but he was a selfish bastard, and he wasn't going to let anyone else have the tiny man. All he could hope for was that he didn't destroy them both.

Twitch turned at that moment with tears shimmering in his eyes, and the most beautiful smile Crave ever saw. Yeah, there was no fucking way he was giving Twitch up.

Twitch would be his in every way, but first, he had to figure out how the fuck to do that.

10 CRAVE WAS BEING WEIRD

Twitch adjusted his ear buds, turned the volume up louder to drive out the real world. The bass seemed to vibrate in his chest as he moved his hips to the beat. He sang along as he continued to pick up Crave's room. It was a day early, but he was bored, and everything else was done. Crave headed out with the Twirled Crew for their weekly Sunday run. Hunter was locked in his room working on some secret project. Psycho was still asleep, and he didn't have a death wish to bother the man. Bull was out in his workshop, so he pretty much had the house to himself.

Crave was a slob. Clothes littered his floor. The man didn't know the meaning of making a damn bed. It didn't help the man was going to spend a fortune in lube. Twitch threw another empty bottle in the trash. He couldn't admit he was happy about the fact condoms hadn't been on Crave's list in a while.

Crave still wasn't bringing anyone home and he always came straight back to the house from work. The man's behavior was weird lately and even seemed to be making an attempt at being nicer. Which was kind of creepy. It just wasn't the Crave he'd known these last four years.

He straightened to fluff Crave's pillows, the scent of man, shampoo and soap were strong. Twitch almost brought it to his nose just to inhale. Shaking his hands violently, Twitch placed the pillow back on the bed. He turned to smooth wrinkles from the bedspread and almost screamed at finding Crave standing in the doorway. Jerking the ear buds out he glared at Crave. "I thought you were gone for the day?"

Crave didn't say a word just stared at him until Twitch started to feel uncomfortable. He spun away to throw the sheets on top of the basket. There was an old t-shirt, well-worn and soft that he'd eyed for almost two weeks. Today it was his.

"You're off your schedule," Crave's voice came from too close behind him.

"Hunter is working on some project and told me to forget about it this week. He's obsessively neat, so I never have much to do." Twitch knew he was probably rambling, but the heat of Crave's big body was soaking into his back. He tried to pretend everything was normal and he wasn't about to lose his shit. "Also I was bored. I cleaned the house yesterday and put together casseroles to throw in the oven for dinner the rest of the week."

"I forgot my wallet."

Crave's warmth disappeared, and Twitch finally breathed easier as he turned. Crave's long strides took him to the dresser. The denim lovingly conformed to a muscled ass and massive thick thighs. Even though all the men he worked around were built on a scale that didn't deviate from huge, Crave always seemed larger. He worked out with his weights out in the barn and beat the hell out of the heavy bag just about every day.

Crave's biceps were the size of Twitch's thighs. He couldn't have a healthy sex life, so he had no business looking at anything on Crave.

"Going to meet back up with the Twirled Crew?"

"I don't know."

"What the hell is wrong with you? You've been weird lately, even for you."

"Nothing."

"Oh, there's the cranky Crave I know."

"I'm trying here okay," Crave hissed without turning around. "This shit isn't easy for me."

"What isn't? Are you seeing—" Twitch bent and jerked the basket up, he didn't want to finish that question.

"No, I'm not seeing or fucking anyone."

He felt like an ass for being relieved. When he'd moved in, he'd learned quick he was going to be living with a lot of healthy, sexually active men. Twitch slowly moved passed his discomfort and except for harmless flirting he'd never made it onto anyone's hookup radar. He'd gotten the support of the Twirled Crew, and only Bull knew the full story of his past. Twitch gave Crave the abridged version.

It wasn't like his parents physically harmed him. He'd never received a spanking growing up or even a slap in the heat of a fight. Well until he'd hit the retreats and high school and he'd been the target of every bully in his vicinity. He wondered what it would be like to have someone touch him, hell, he'd give anything for a kiss.

"Hey, what's this?" Crave's rough fingertips slipped beneath his chin.

Crave's other hand traced the fringe of his lashes and Twitch realized he was crying. Shit, couldn't he go one day without embarrassing himself?

"Nothing." Twitch tried to jerk away, but Crave's thumb and forefinger pinched his chin to keep him in place.

"Don't lie to me, we made a damn deal."

He'd tried to forget that so-called deal for two weeks. Twitch didn't want the strong man to see him when he was at his lowest. The nights where he couldn't seem to find his way.

"That was if I was feeling lost, I'm not—"

"Then why the tears?"

"I was thinking that's all."

"About what?"

"What normal would be like." It was close enough to the truth because Twitch sucked at lying. And no matter what everyone else said, he didn't possess a poker face.

"Normal sucks, boring, complete waste of fucking time."

He smiled and pushed at Crave's stomach with the basket. "Of course you'd say that."

Crave let go of his chin and took the basket from his hands, Crave twisted his body and set it on the bed.

"Listen, people all have their own shit to deal with. Fucked up childhoods. Some bastard who wouldn't take no for an answer. A cheating ex. A screwed up doctrine that makes people feel inferior or ashamed."

He reached for Crave and fisted his hands in the sides of his t-shirt. "The programs were hell, and then the jocks in high school thought I'd be a great punching bag."

"Got a yearbook," Crave asked.

It took a minute to get his mind around the question, and he rolled his eyes.

"You're not hunting down the dumb asses from when I was in school."

"I could."

"I'm sure, but you're not."

Other than Crave's lack of impulse control the guy wasn't bad. He had his quirks like the rest of the crew. His were a bit more extreme, although as much as he loved Psycho, the man was worse than Crave. The very scope of that statement was terrifying. Twitch knew though that there wasn't much they wouldn't do for each other. If you were in trouble, the Twirled and Brawlers crew were the ones to have as backup.

"Why do you people live to ruin my fun?"

There was the cute pout Crave was famous for when his plans for violence were impeded.

"Because you're beautiful and I don't think you'd do well in a confined environment such as prison. They also have a lot of rules."

He forced himself to not flinch or tense as strong arms wrapped around him. Twitch laid his head on Crave's chest. The man's bristly chin rested on the top of his head.

"That is true, and I don't do well with those. This is nice," Crave whispered.

"It's a bit weird."

"Weird?"

"You've never touched me, and now I'm getting hugs."

That along with the other strange things going on with Crave caused him to worry a bit. He'd heard what happened while he stayed at Drake's and Bull's threat to send Crave packing. Twitch didn't want Crave to lose his home. He'd known before Crave moved there he'd constantly moved around the US, Canada, and Mexico. Eight years was a long time to stay in one spot after never staying in a place more than a few nights. "Bull wouldn't kick you out, you know that, right?"

"That isn't what this is about. I'm an asshole and drove you from your home." Crave's hands tugged gently at his hair until he tipped his head back. "You always have a keep away sign burning bright like the neon over your precious bar."

"My parents were never affectionate."

"No hugs growing up?"

"Open displays of affection were considered plebeian," he answered with a roll of his eyes.

"Breaking out the big words."

"Do you need a dictionary," Twitch asked with a smile.

"Yeah."

"Vulgar, is that better?"

"And to think when I met you I thought you were all sweet…" Crave's arms tightened around him and then eased up a bit, "and shy."

"Those days ended when I started living with y'all."

"Bound to happen. You planning to steal another shirt today?"

"They're comfortable to sleep in," Twitch said, pulling away.

"I wasn't complaining, I got plenty. Which one this time?"

"Your old navy blue one that's faded to almost gray."

"Now, I see why you do my laundry with yours, easier to swipe."

"Exactly, now speaking of laundry, I have to get ours done, then get dinner started."

"What about a ride tonight," Crave asked he turned to pick up the basket.

"If I get everything done."

"I'll help."

"You're offering to do housework, are you okay? You're not dying are ya?"

"Shut up and take the offer before I change my mind. I'll ride out on my own without you."

"Bastard," Twitch muttered and grabbed the basket from Crave. He headed for the door and sensed Crave close behind him. Crave was being weird, but it wasn't a bad kind. The hug had been friendly. He hadn't felt threatened. They'd had a conversation without fighting once.

"Get moving, you'll never get done."

"Fine, but you're buying me ice cream," he said with a glance over his shoulder, then turned back to descend the stairs.

"Deal."

He knew the possibility of them being more than friends was nonexistent, but friends would be nice. He just wished he felt it would be enough. He loved the man, crazy and all, but that would be between him, Drake and Paul.

11 TWITCH WAS FORBIDDEN TO DANCE IN PUBLIC

Crave's crankiness soared to homicidal. He hadn't slept thinking about the way Twitch's pants had molded to his rounded ass or the way his hips moved to whatever song he'd been listening to. His man was forbidden to dance in public. No one was going to see that but him. The long ride he'd taken the little man on hadn't helped either. Twitch had wrapped his body around his much bigger one. If all that shit hadn't been bad enough he'd had to watch Twitch innocently lick ice cream and Crave's mind only went deeper in the gutter.

He was a fucking moron getting jealous over a damn ice cream cone.

Crave stayed near the door as he observed Twitch sitting on the bar. Hunter was leaned back between his legs and Twitch was working on braiding the man's long hair. Hunter was tapping away on his phone and Twitch was laughing as he read it.

"Oh, don't forget you almost dropped that case of beer on your head," Twitch barely got the sentence out between his giggles.

"Fuck, I was trying to forget that one."

Crave couldn't take it, he needed to be near Twitch. "What the hell are y'all doing?"

"Hunter keeps a record of how many times a night he attempts to injure or kill himself."

"Really," Crave asked.

"There's gotta be a quota on fuck ups one person can make. I have to be getting near mine."

Hunter was a good-looking kid, early twenties with a handsome young face, but the man really could fuck up breathing. They gave him shit about it, but it was just to make sure he felt included. He was the newest member of the crew. Only working with them for six months or so. Hunter didn't really talk about himself and typically stayed to himself, yet he and Twitch became friends. Unlike with other men who got too close to Twitch he didn't get jealous of Hunter. The two men didn't even flirt.

"You'd think so, wouldn't ya?" Crave spun and plopped down on the stool beside Hunter. He automatically lifted his arm to lie along Twitch's thigh.

Crave was trying to be affectionate. He didn't know if it was working or not, but at least he was trying. That had to be worth at least something.

"Oh, what about when you almost got your dick stuck in your zipper before work."

"Shit, I forgot about that one," Hunter cussed and started tapping again.

"And how the fuck would you know that?"

"I'm surprised you didn't hear him yell." Twitch snorted. "Uncut shouldn't go commando especially if you're accident prone."

"I'm not fucking hearing this," Crave rumbled deep in his chest. He tried to calm himself down.

"You didn't know Hunter tends to sleepwalk about once a week or so. I told him he needs to wear clothes to bed. I don't need to see that. I swear I thought I'd found proof of Sasquatch."

"I'm not that—"

"Oh you so are, I swear it would look bigger if you trimmed."

Hunter turned his head and in the process pulled his hair. "Ouch, dammit."

"Another one," Twitch squealed.

"You're having too much fun with this," Hunter muttered as he began typing again. "Can't you do something with him?"

Crave turned his head to find Hunter staring at him with an imploring look.

"Come on, Pipsqueak, quit being mean to Hunter." Crave stood, grabbed Twitch around the waist and tossed the man over his shoulder.

"Hey, quit manhandling the help," Elijah said with a huge smile.

"Apparently he's being a little shit to Hunter."

"That's normal, did you tell him to add the skid down the basement steps?"

"Dammit," Hunter yelled.

Everyone started laughing. Poor kid, they really needed to do something about him. "Do you think if we wrap him in bubble wrap he'll hurt himself less?"

"No, he'd suffocate," Twitch's muffled reply was filled with glee.

"Twitch, be nice, what's gotten into you," Elijah asked.

"Oh, that might be my fault," Crave answered.

"What the hell did you do?"

"I gave him chocolate covered coffee beans."

"Are you insane," Scary bellowed. "Have you seen him on sugar, now you throw coffee beans on top of it. Oh, he's all yours. Your responsibility."

That was all right with him, but he didn't say it out loud. They'd only reached the hugs stage and maybe casual touches. Okay, Twitch draped over his shoulder was something else, but he wasn't protesting. Which was strange?

"What are you doing," he asked as he felt fingertips rubbing the fabric of his t-shirt at the small of his back.

"When did you get this t-shirt?"

"Last week, why?"

"No reason."

The stroking continued like a kid with a security blanket. It was like he was content just to hang there moving his fingers over the fabric. Twitch was obsessed with his clothes, no, just his t-shirts. It had to be more than they were comfortable to sleep in.

"Is it going to come up missing?"

"Definitely, but you won't know when and you won't know where."

Crave nearly dropped Twitch when he lost it at the sound the accurate impression of a villain laugh. Okay, mental note: No more coffee or sugar for Twitch.

He noticed the room was quiet and he scanned the occupants to find them staring at them with a little too much speculation in their gazes. Nothing was going on between them, not that he didn't fucking want there to be something. Crave knew he needed to be slow and subtle, two things he wasn't good at, but for Twitch he wanted to try.

"I'm taking the fiend home."

"Be careful that he doesn't bounce off the back of your bike," Elijah warned.

"Never happen," Crave assured them. He'd never do anything to hurt Twitch.

Although he knew he'd hurt Twitch's feelings over the years. Yelled at him too much. Probably even stifled him some, but it was just because he didn't want the little man hurt. Mostly, he wanted to make Twitch his.

He started to move toward the door.

"Hey, my bag."

Crave stopped to turn only to find Hunter handing the pink backpack to Twitch.

"Thanks, Sasq—"

"I swear all your favorite t-shirts will come up missing," Hunter warned.

"Don't be mean, they're all soft and warm."

Crave heard the pout in Twitch's voice, and he continued toward the door. He pushed the exit door and stepped out into the chilly night. The deputy who was usually parked across the street was driving through the parking lot. He slowly pulled to a stop.

"Everything okay here," A deep voice came from the darkened interior.

Okay, it probably looked suspicious to be fireman carrying someone through a parking lot at almost 3 a.m. He shook his head at the mental picture.

"Yeah, just taking my boy home," Crave answered.

Twitch's body slid to the side and Crave looked down to see Twitch peering around his side.

"I'm not his boy, now, home, James, I feel a sugar crash coming."

The deputy laughed. "Y'all have a good night."

"Thanks, you too."

The cruiser pulled out of the parking lot and onto the road heading back toward town.

"You almost got us arrested," Twitch protested.

"Doubt it."

Crave slid Twitch off his shoulder and gently set him on his feet. He looked down into Twitch's face, and the man was beautiful. His features were small and feminine, soft, and normally that wasn't something he went for, but Twitch was perfection to him.

"You know I can drive to work, right," Twitch asked as he lifted his helmet from where it hung on the handlebars.

"Yeah, but we're all coming to the same place."

Twitch let out a cute huff and set his half helmet on top of his head. Crave reached forward and secured the chin strap. Twitch's skin was silky soft against his fingers. He stepped back to put on his own helmet and mounted the bike.

Crave held out his hand to help Twitch up and nearly groaned as the man wiggled against his back until there was no space left between their bodies. His cock hardened and pushed painfully at the back of his zipper. He took deep even breaths as he tried to get his body to calm. It wasn't helping much when Twitch's arms came around him, and he started repeating the circles on his abs that he'd done earlier to his lower back.

With another deep breath, he started the bike and slowly pulled out of the parking lot.

He'd never noticed how truly touchy feely Twitch was, but looking back there were hints. The way he'd ruffled the hair on Zerk's arm. All the hugs Twitch and Bull shared. Even the way Hunter let Twitch brush and braid his hair when Crave knew the man generally kept it loose. Everyone took care of Twitch, but Crave wanted that to be his job.

He didn't want Twitch to go to Lucky and Priest for the nights he needed to be held. Crave wanted to be the one Twitch came to for his cuddling and need for affection. It was new and odd territory for him. In the past, he was the one men came to for a brutal fuck, some pain with their pleasure, but he wasn't what Twitch thought. Yeah, he liked his men submissive, yet he wasn't a Dom. He just liked rough, to be in control, and he wanted his partners vocal in their pleasure.

When the time came, he wondered if he could do that? Make Twitch lose control enough to let go entirely. First, though he needed to get Twitch comfortable with him. With that he was lost, he'd never been with a man like Twitch before, and that meant he had to try something new. He had to be patient, shit, he was sure as fuck that wasn't one of his virtues, and he had very few of those.

12 WHERE WAS CRAVE TAKING HIM?

Twitch hugged his travel mug of coffee to his chest as he attempted to play keep away with Crave. "Mine," he squealed and bent to try to hug his body around it.

One minute he was standing there and the next Crave hauled him off his feet. That wasn't emasculating at all, being held by the waist while curled into a fetal position protecting coffee. It didn't help he was wearing pink pajama bottoms with kittens on them and one of Crave's t-shirts that hung on him like a dress.

"Give it to me, after last night, no, Twitch, no," Crave's chest rumbled against his back.

Crave might be bigger, but Twitch was stubborn. There was no way the man was getting his coffee, extra strong with extra sugar and mocha creamer.

"Mine." Twitch kicked out one leg and skimmed Crave's hip.

"Watch it, you little shit, you're about to ruin my sex life."

"That would be a shame since it's probably your only good feature."

"What the fuck are you two doing," Bull roared from the doorway.

He froze and felt Crave do the same, he almost snorted at the mental picture of the scene before Bull.

"He's trying to steal my coffee," he pouted.

"He bounced on my bed for an hour last night before he settled down."

Twitch snorted.

"Sonuvabitch, will you two behave? Crave, put him down."

He waited to be dropped, but Crave set him gently on his feet. As soon as Twitch as free he ran to hide behind Bull. He peeked around the man's arm and stuck out his tongue.

Three, two, one—Crave chin dropped, and the relaxation breathing began.

Twitch loudly slurped his coffee, and it earned him a glare that promised retribution. He didn't know why he was playing with fire. Maybe he'd consumed too much coffee. Crave was volatile on a good day. Poking the cranky ursine beast was like playing with a nuclear bomb ready to explode. He really should be terrified of what Crave could do if he lost his temper, but he wasn't afraid of the man.

"It's not even noon yet, what the hell are you two doing up?"

"Crave made me get up. Said he was taking me somewhere, but won't tell me where. I wanted to leave a note in case someone needed to search for my body later."

"I'm not going to hurt you. I found this place I'd thought you'd like. It was going to be a nice surprise. I changed my fucking mind," Crave's voice was dangerously low.

Oh shit, he darted around Bull and thrust his mug at him. "Hold this, guard it with your life." He jogged until he stepped in front of Crave to bar his escape. "Where were you gonna take me?" He smiled sweetly and batted his lashes. It always worked on Bull, so it was worth a try.

"Nope, I'm going back to bed."

Crave stepped forward, and Twitch threw up his hands to push against his stomach. Damn, he resisted the temptation to knead the insanely hard ridges of Crave's abs. He knew there were eight of them. Twitch counted them a thousand times since the first time he'd seen Crave shirtless.

If only he knew what to do with him, hell, if he didn't panic at the thought of doing something with anyone.

"It's ruined, I'm—"

"Please." Twitch dug deep and brought out the pout, add some quivering. Add a bit of aw shucks twisting from side to side and a sad, contemplative look at his laced fingers. Five, four, three, two—

"Aw, fuck, don't do that."

Score, Twitch held the pose even as he did a mental victory dance like a stripper on a pole. "I just wanted to know where you were taking me." Any more resistance and Twitch would cry, just a few tears are all it would take.

"Ya always look jealous when we take off to swim out at Tank's place, and I know why now. I found this spot and thought you'd like to go."

"Really, but..." Twitched raised his hand and stroked his right side. "They're ugly."

"It's just us, and I don't care."

"Okay." He bounced in place and ran around Crave to grab his coffee from a scowling Bull.

"Be careful, Twitch."

"I know, but I'll be okay."

"If not, just text with whatever, I still have your GPS Tracker on my phone."

"You're way too paranoid. It's Crave."

"Yeah, that's why." Bull didn't say anything else and turned to head back to his room.

"How long do I have to get ready?"

"Whenever. I already packed a picnic, and my pack is next to the door."

"Fifteen and I'll be ready."

Twitch ran off to find something he could swim in. He'd never brought trunks, but he was sure he had a pair of his underwear that would work. One thing he didn't know if it would work or not was getting shirtless in from of Crave. He wasn't muscular or toned, his body was average and scarred. Shit, he wasn't going to think about it. Twitch was going to focus on spending the afternoon with Crave. That's all he could do.

■■■■

It was beautiful, the path in was barely wide enough for Crave's bike, but they finally made it. He stood at the water's edge as he listened to Crave moving around behind him. Twitch darted a glance over his shoulder to find Crave spreading out a blanket.

"It's great, how did you find it?"

"Tank. He said it was a little out of the way, but he used to come here to think before he met Elijah. We rode out here last week so he could show me. Like it?"

"It's perfect."

He plopped down onto the ground and started unlacing his boots. He removed them and his socks, pulled the legs of his jeans up and stood walking into the water. It was cold against his feet and lower legs.

"You can strip down and get in if you want."

"This is—"

"I brought you here so you could get comfortable and swim."

"It's not exactly pretty under my clothes."

"Come on, Twitch, I saw the scars. It ain't like I don't know they're there."

Twitch was being an idiot, but Lucky and Priest saw him without his clothes, Trouble saw him shirtless for his nipple piercings. They didn't look at him differently, but they weren't Crave. He'd fallen in love with the weird man over the years.

He kept his back to Crave and reached the bottom of his t-shirt. Twitch licked his dry lips and slowly lifted the shirt up and off. He held it tight in his hands.

"Turn around," Crave ordered.

"Do I have'ta?"

"Please."

It was still weird to hear Crave say that. The man demanded, he barely said please or thank you, and definitely not to him. He turned until he faced Crave and the man was right there.

Large hands reached out and tugged the cotton from his hands.

"Why?"

"Sex is supposed to be natural. Two people showing each other how they physically feel about each other. Attraction. Need. Love. My parents made it into a sin. An act to be endured. Puberty turned into hell. If I couldn't feel the pleasure, I needed to feel something."

"But you don't think that anymore, right?"

"I don't know. I still panic, and the anxiety gets the best of me. My shrink says I need positive reinforcement. That's where Lucky and Priest came in. I could sleep cuddled between them."

"But what about finding a man?"

"No." Twitch shook his head.

"Why not? Shit, you've been around the Twirled and Brawler crews, ain't nothing more natural than sex."

"That is true. I'm passed my discomfort of other people having sex, hearing it, but I can't even get myself off. Bull talked—"

"I'd prefer not knowing about you, Bull and sex talks."

Twitch snorted. "He's been like a dad to me since I started working at Brawlers and let me move in. Car living was—"

"You were homeless?"

"Yeah, for about six months. My parents thought I'd shamed them with my behavior. They stopped paying my tuition, my apartment and canceled all my cards. My job at a coffee house in Atlanta didn't exactly cover my rent, bills, and tuition."

"I imagine not." Crave stepped closer.

Twitch held his breath as Crave lifted his right hand and stroked his palm over his left side. Crave gently caressed down the even row of scars from under his right pectoral down his ribs to where they disappeared beneath his jeans. Twitch grabbed Crave's hand to stop him from going lower. His body trembled at the strange sensation, it was a tingling that bloomed beneath his skin. It wasn't unpleasant.

"Off with the jeans and into the water and then we'll have something to eat."

Crave lifted his arms over his head and reached back to tug his shirt over his head. A broad, powerful chest with muscular, rounded pecs covered in dark blond hair. His nipples were dark disks with pebbled tips. The thick hair thinned over the unnaturally deep cut of his abs. Did ordinary men even have stomachs like that? The hair thickly flared back out under his outie belly button and disappeared beneath the low hung waist of his jeans.

"Problem?"

He covered his perusal with humor. "You need to lay off the steroids."

"Ha ha, funny man, in the water before I toss you in."

"No need to be defensive, I just heard it shrinks your—"

He giggled as Crave growled and lunged at him. Twitch was quicker and got out of his way, darting around him to step back up onto the bank. With his back turned he undid his jeans and pushed them down, the boy shorts didn't leave much to the imagination, and of course, they were pink. He didn't have much choice in swimming attire.

Before he talked himself out of it, he spun and took off running into the water. "Shit, that's cold." It hadn't felt that chilly with just his feet submerged. When he got deep enough, he dunked his head under and tilted back when he broke the surface.

He realized his mistake too soon. Crave's muscled backside was on full display. It was an ass unseen outside of models or bodybuilders. Crave shook out a pair of trunks and bent over to step into them, then straightened as he slid them up his massive legs.

There was no way in hell he would be able to handle that man. Not even if he wasn't completely fucked up in the head Crave would intimidate him. The man was gorgeous and dangerous, he'd even recently had moments where he was nice. Like today, he'd thought about Twitch's comfort.

He leaned back to start floating and stared up at the bright blue sky. A gentle breeze blew across his wet skin, the ends of his hair tickled his shoulders.

"Worth coming out for." Crave's breath teased his ear.

"Definitely, thank you."

"You're welcome."

He turned his head and started to sink beneath the water, but strong arms cradled him. Twitch had tensed for a minute before he relaxed. It was surreal, and he didn't understand what was happening, but he was enjoying the new friendship with Crave. He knew he couldn't have more, he wasn't Crave's type, but it was enough for him. It would have to be.

13 CRAVE HAD COMPANY

Crave awakened as he sensed he wasn't alone but kept his eyes closed. The hinges of his door squeaked as it opened and closed, then the soft shuffling of feet moved over the hardwood floors.

"Crave," Twitch's small voice whispered in the darkness.

He cracked his eyes open and turned to find Twitch standing beside his bed. A blanket wrapped tight around his slim body, his bare shoulders exposed.

"You okay?"

"Can I sleep with you?" Insecurity thickened Twitch's usually sweet tone.

He didn't answer just grabbed the covers and lifted them. Twitch dropped the blanket, and for a minute Crave took in all his smooth skin. He nearly groaned at the sexy, tiny boy shorts that stretched low across Twitch's prominent hipbones.

Crave turned to his side as Twitch dove between the covers.

"Fuck, you're cold," Crave huffed.

Twitch didn't say anything just wiggled against him until Crave swore there wasn't even a breath of space between their bodies. Twitch's hair teased his chin and Crave tucked the covers around the smaller man.

"You okay," Crave asked.

He roughly rubbed Twitch's back trying to get some warmth into Twitch's smaller body.

"Not really, I'm cold."

"I can tell, wanna talk?"

"What's your favorite color?"

"Really?"

"Uh huh." Twitch nodded to punctuate.

"Green." It was the exact shade of Twitch's eyes.

"Figured you for black."

"Second favorite." Because black was the color of Twitch's hair. "Now, what about you?"

"Blue, I've always liked bright blue, like the sky on a clear day."

"Good choice."

Twitch's cold toes rubbed against his calves. He swore the man had to be cold-blooded. Crave held Twitch tighter. Twitch snugged his petite body closer and stroked his smooth cheek against Crave's chest. Fuck, it wasn't time for a hard-on, but his dick didn't have any intention of listening to him. He tried to shift his hips away, but Twitch followed. It seemed like the man didn't want any space between them at all.

If they had a normal relationship and Twitch understood what Crave wanted from him, he'd show Twitch he didn't need to fear sex. Crave reminded himself he'd struck the deal for Twitch to come to him to keep his man out of Lucky and Priest's bed. He admitted his selfishness and knew it would be hard to keep shit innocent, but this was going to be damn near impossible.

"Can I ask you something personal?"

"I reserve the right not to answer," Twitch said.

"Deal, have you ever done anything with a guy?"

Twitch sighed heavily, his warm breath teasing Crave's skin. The other man remained quiet for so long Crave thought Twitch wouldn't answer.

"I tried dating in college, but I panicked like some Victorian Virgin when the guy would lean in to kiss me. I couldn't get away fast enough, suffice it to say I never got an offer for a second date."

Shit, not only a virgin but never been kissed either. Wow, that was unknown territory.

"If you fucking didn't have all the hang-ups about sex, what would you want?"

Small, slender fingers drew circles on the indent at the base of Crave's spine. His impulse control ran at minimal, and Twitch's touch wasn't helping. Twitch leaned his slight weight against him.

"I know I should say—"

"This isn't about what you should say, what the fuck would you want?"

"A kiss, is that weird? I'm twenty-five, shouldn't I want to just have sex?"

"Shit, when I was—" Crave groaned, he was showing his age. "You got all this shit twisted up in your head. Anybody can fuck. It's easy enough to get, but a kiss is something else."

"Why?"

"I don't know, sometimes hookups don't require a kiss, it's all about the getting off. I ain't saying it's always like that."

"Is it that way for you?"

"Used to be." Until you, but he didn't say it. Twitch finally came to him, and he couldn't fuck that up the first night. "Do you trust me?"

"What?"

"You want a kiss, I won't push, and we're friends."

"You'd kiss me?"

"Yeah." Crave pulled back and raised his hand to lay it on Twitch's cheek. His hand was so big he slipped his thumb under Twitch's chin to tilt his face up. Twitch's gaze focused on his mouth. The pink tip of Twitch's peeked out to lick his lips. Crave suppressed a groan.

He lowered his head until his lips barely brushed Twitch's and he held still. Twitch needed to make the next move. Pushing him wasn't an option. One kiss, he could deal with that without losing control.

"It's up to you, you're in control," he whispered, and his lips rubbed against Twitch's.

"I don't know."

"Do what feels right."

"Can I touch you?"

"Yeah," Crave answered, he steeled himself for whatever happened next. He'd never just kissed someone before. A kiss always ended in a rough fuck and a quick goodbye. He wanted the fuck, but not the *so long see ya later* ending.

Stay relaxed, keep your cool, Butler, Crave mentally ordered himself. That would be easier said than done. Going from one day of not allowing himself to touch

Twitch even in a casual way to fucking cuddling with no expectation of, well, a fuck.

The warmth of Twitch's small hands hovered barely an inch from his chest. If he took one deep breath Twitch would touch him. He suppressed the lure and swore to himself he'd let Twitch make the first move.

He watched Twitch's expression searching for any sign the man was close to panicking. Twitch wasn't moving, he seemed to barely be breathing, Crave almost started to pull away to put distance between them yet stopped as Twitch's small, soft hands settled on his chest. He drew in a sharp breath at the feel of his man freely touching him.

"Did I do something wrong," Twitch's voice soft and uncertain.

"No." Crave surprised by the roughness of his voice.

Crave muscles flexed as Twitch massaged his chest with his slim fingers. He resisted the urge to arch and push harder into Twitch's hesitant touch.

This might turn out to be his biggest fuck up ever. Twitch's slim fingers combed through the thick hair on his chest, and the slight pain of the tug caused him to involuntarily push into Twitch's touch. Fuck, his dick hardened and pushed into the softness of Twitch's stomach.

He wrapped his hand around the back of Twitch's thigh and stroked upward until the side of his fingers met the curve of one perfect cheek. He froze waiting for Twitch to push him away. It was a complete dumb ass move.

Twitch tilted his chin and brought their mouths together. Crave forced himself to be still. It needed to be Twitch's show. The tentative kiss was awkward and proved Twitch's inexperience, but he'd never felt anything half as good. It scared the fuck out him he'd be Twitch's first everything, kiss, fuck. He might have done something right in his life.

Twitch's lips were gentle as fuck. Twitch's mouth sucked at his top lip, then the bottom one, Crave slanted his head to deepen the kiss. He parted his lips to trace the soft seam of Twitch's mouth with the tip of his tongue. Twitch gasped, and he took advantage, he slowly thrust his tongue inside. He stroked Twitch's as he lifted the smaller man's thigh over his.

The man's slender arms twined around his neck, and Crave took it as an invitation. He used his weight to press Twitch's back into the mattress. Crave flexed his arm and drew Twitch's leg high onto his side. His cock hardened and pushed to Twitch's hip.

He slowly realized Twitch wasn't responding and he opened his eyes to look down into Twitch's pale face.

"Fuck." He instantly rolled to his back and covered his face with his hands. Crave dared a look to find Twitch unnaturally still, and his thin chest jerked with his shaky breaths. Twitch's fingers were absently stroking along the scars on his ribs. Something about that move concerned Crave.

Crave took a huge chance and stretched out his right arm, then laid his hand open on Twitch's stomach. The small muscles contracted under his palm and fingers. Twitch traced the back of his hand with slim, soft fingers.

"Sorry," Crave whispered.

He was hoping Twitch wouldn't run from him. He barely made ground since his fuck up, and he didn't want to take several steps back only to work to gain Twitch's trust again.

"That was…interesting."

He didn't know why but his lips curved into a smile.

"I'm not sure if I should be insulted or not that a kiss from me was just interesting."

"As first ones go—"

"Yeah?"

"Maybe we can try again…later."

"Okay, I can do later."

"I should go back to my own room."

"Naw, you're good." Crave stretched his arm out farther and tugged until Twitch completely rested against his side. He shifted until he could slip his arm under Twitch's head. "Just go to sleep."

Twitch wasn't running so that had to be a good sign. Although he wasn't so sure about Twitch's reaction to the kiss. Maybe he really was in the friend zone with Twitch, and he shouldn't get his hopes too high. Shit, what if someone like Lucky or Priest were more Twitch's type. Fuck, that would suck. He'd lose his man to a hyper hippie, just fucking great.

"Quit thinking so hard, you'll give yourself a headache," Twitch teased.

"I don't like you."

"I don't like you either."

He chuckled at the smile in Twitch's voice. Hell, he wasn't such a fuck up after all.

14 CRAVE NEEDED A LEASH AND WHY DID THAT SOUND LIKE A PLAN?

Twitch could quickly kill the blond bastard with a smile on his face. He silently screamed as he tried to ignore Crave staring at him from beside the front exit. The man's attention wasn't new Crave always kept a close eye on him when Twitch worked. It seemed more annoying lately.

He sighed heavily and tensed as a large arm came to rest on his shoulders. He rolled his eyes as he turned to glance up at Hunter.

"From personal experience, let me assure you, you'd never survive prison."

"Is it that obvious?"

"Definitely. There are worse things in life than being the sole focus of a man like Crave."

"Something you want to tell me, Hunter."

"Fuck no, I'd rather be celibate."

"I think jerking off puts you in abstinence category, celibate is something else."

"Smart ass, you know Crave has a huge thing for you."

"I'd rather not think about what's in his pants." Twitch grinned as Hunter choked out a laugh.

"And to think I thought of you as an innocent among the hedonists."

"You live with them as long as I have and see how…what am I saying, you're as bad as them."

"Don't lump me in, there's been no screaming from my room."

"That is true, why is that?"

"You've met me, right?"

"Okay, you're a bit awkward, but not all that bad."

"Yeah, dating just doesn't work for me."

"Then don't date, as far as I know sex doesn't always have to involve commitment or a relationship beyond knowing condom size and lube preference."

"You've been fucking hanging out with Crave too much."

"Take that back," Twitch screeched as he spun away and showed off his unimpressive, tiny fists.

"Oh, my fucking—" Hunter bent at the waist as he laughed his fool head off, "don't ever—" Hunter choked on his own spit.

"Good, I hope you choke to death."

"What the fuck is going on here," Crave's growled.

"I'm waiting for him to turn blue so I can toss him out back."

"Hunter, what did you do to him," Crave demanded.

"What did I…" Hunter cleared his throat. "He wished for my death."

"That's why I asked what the fuck you did."

"A beautiful, innocent face gets you off the hook for everything—"

"Nope," Twitch popped the P. "I get in just as much trouble as someone as homely as you."

"Twitch."

He turned his head as Crave barked his name, "Yes?"

"You're asking for a spanking."

"What did I do?" Twitch lowered his lashes to conceal his eyes and let his lip start to quiver.

"No, that's not," Crave growled. "It's not going to work, dammit, baby, stop that."

"But I didn't do anything. Hunter was mean to me. He even said I was hanging out with you too much." He glanced at Hunter to find the man wearing a panicked expression.

"Are you trying to get me killed, you little shit," Hunter hissed, and started backing away.

Twitch cut off a giggle at the scene of Hunter ducking backward under the apron and nearly slamming his head into the thick wood counter. Hunter flipped him off. The man was a fatal accident waiting to happen, but he loved the crazy klutz.

He turned his attention back to Crave. Twitch gave the big man his sweetest smile.

"You're trouble."

"What did I—"

"Don't even try it."

Twitch rolled his eyes. "You haven't attempted to kill anyone tonight, are you feeling okay?" He bent at the waist and stretched until he could rest his forearms on the bar.

"Smartass," Crave rumbled.

Shit, Twitch almost retreated as Crave rested his arms on either side of Twitch's and Twitch let his gaze fall to

Crave's firm, full lips. He'd analyzed their kiss a hundred times in the past few days. He was still embarrassed by the after, interesting, did he actually say Crave's kiss was merely interesting?

Twitch hadn't panicked that in itself was amazing, but it came nowhere near the butterflies that had exploded in his stomach. Crave's weight on top of him was perfect. The big man hadn't pushed for more than the kiss even when Crave seemed to lose control before he caught himself. Twitch still didn't know what he felt. He loved the blond bastard. The kiss was something else, Crave said it was just something between friends.

"What's got you thinking so fucking hard," Crave asked.

"Nothing."

"I'll let it go, but don't lie to me again."

"Don't be an asshole."

"And that's strange for me?"

Twitched rolled his eyes. "No." A movement over Crave's shoulder caught his attention. Fuck. "Trouble at your six."

Crave slowly turned his head to glance back over his shoulder.

The local closeted roughneck stood looking around, Bill and his friends got a little too much booze in them, and they wanted to fight. When he wasn't coming to Brawlers to try his hand at being big and bad, the rumor was he took out his frustrations on Harper.

Harper was the only out Transwoman in Powers. Beautiful, blonde and petite, and sweet as could be, but apparently had shit taste in men. Maybe Bill thought if he fucked Harper, he could pretend he didn't head to Atlanta for a man to hook up with any weekend he could sneak away. Bill's friends must be idiots.

Twitch really needed to have her join him for lunch soon.

"Should I dial 9-1-1, and wait?"

"Naw, we got this, remember to duck down if shit goes south."

"They didn't hire me because I was a Brawler, they hired me because I'm…"

"Don't finish that fucking sentence."

Twitch shrugged and straightened, he casually retreated to lean against the back bar. He reached behind his thigh to press the emergency button that sounded an alarm in Scary and Tank's office.

The tension in the room immediately thickened turning the air oppressive. Bill and his crew were clearly outmatched, but they had more balls than brains. Twitch watched Crave stretch to his full height, and he seemed to get even bigger. The rage and power that was Crave intensified as he prepared for battle. And it would be a battle, Crave like the rest of the Brawlers Crew were the best for a reason.

As Crave smoothly moved forward, Twitch took in the the rest of the crew advancing, Psycho and Bull flanked Bill and his boys from either side of the door. Scary and Tank appeared from the hallway.

The crowd seemed to shrink back leaving the Brawlers in the open. Everyone knew if they were in the way they'd be casualties before the fight ended. Hunter wasn't a fighter either, so the man joined him and leaned back beside him.

"What do you think, I got fifty Psycho has a bigger body count than Crave."

"Make it a hundred."

"Confident in your boyfriend, huh?"

"Shut up and show me the cash," Twitch said.

Hunter turned and dug out two hundred from the tip jar to cover them both. He slapped it down on top of the beer cooler.

As Crave approached Bill. Rule one: Try to talk the asshole down (Not Crave's strong suit.). It was the only rule. Giving the Crew mandates to follow always ended in disaster, so, they kept it simple.

Crave didn't raise his voice, but Twitch saw Bill's nostrils flare and his top lip pulled back as he snarled.

"Another fifty says Bill is stupid enough to throw the first punch," Twitch whispered.

"You know that's a sucker bet, Crave opens his mouth, and everyone wants to knock the fuck out of him."

"True."

Something about Crave in battle-mode was sexy as hell. Twitch wouldn't admit that to anyone, but when Crave was in the ring—Twitch cut off that thought. Hunter would call him on a blush in a second.

Twitch noticed the slight shift of Bill's shoulder and Crave quickly blocked the punch. That's all it took for all Hell to break loose. The Brawlers converged, and customers skirted the edges of the room toward the nearest exits. A few felt brave and joined in the fray.

Crave's cold laughter rose above the cacophony of war. Twitch searched him out and shook his head, Crave effortlessly toyed with Bill.

That's when a movement caught his attention. An old opponent of Crave's was attempting to come up behind him. Neon flashed off the steel of a blade. No way would Crave hear him in the chaos. Not fucking happening, Twitch snatched a bat from the hooks under the bar.

He easily avoided Hunter who yelled his name. Twitch quickly moved under the apron a few feet to his right. The scarred, wooden bat in his hand felt heavy and cumbersome as he tightened his fists around the base. Twitch quickened his steps, his heart pounded in an erratic rhythm, and he felt the first stirrings of a panic attack.

The bastard had his arm drawn back and was a mere few feet from Crave. He remembered all the years of the dreaded batting practice. Twitch's heart nearly stopped when Crave stumbled backward, and the man behind him started to swing his arm forward. Twitch yelled as he swung and aimed for the bastard's knees.

The man hollered and collapsed to the floor. Twitch jerked his attention away from the fallen man and back to Crave as a huge fist stopped inches from connecting with his cheek.

Twitch squeaked and raised his hands, letting the bat fall to the floor.

It wasn't the threat of the almost-hit that forced all the air from his lungs, no it was Crave's tanned face turning ashen and Crave retreated. His fist was frozen in mid-air.

"Baby, I…" Crave uncurled his fingers, then started to reach for Twitch, but stopped.

Tears shimmered in the man's eyes. He took a step forward but stopped when Crave moved backward.

"Crave, it's—"

He barely got the words out before Crave spun and took off at a run. Twitch hollered for Crave, but the door already slammed shut behind Crave. That's when a thought hit him. The man's past and the greatest fear Crave carried.

Twitch fought as he was grabbed from behind and spun. There wasn't an almost-hit, pain radiated as a forearm connected with his jaw and everything went black.

15 MOM, DO YOU REMEMBER ME?

Crave scrubbed his sweaty palms on his denim covered thighs and tried to calm the nausea churning in his stomach. He pushed a long breath through his compressed lips and reached for the tarnished knob on the plain white door. As he turned it the lock squeaked and he gently shoved the door open, he made note the door stuck in the upper right corner.

He grew angry as he realized he was prolonging the inevitable. Crave stepped into the cheery, brightly lit room, and there she was. Annette Butler.

For a minute, he didn't see his mom as she was now.

Nettie used to have the most beautiful, dark blonde hair, the same shade as his and no matter the hell she'd lived through she'd always smiled for him. Full-figured with a weakness for these gaudy flowered sundresses. His earliest memory was being held up and spun, her smile brighter as she watched him while he flailed his limbs and squealed.

She'd be disappointed in the man he'd become. Nettie of the present was so much different, one side of her ashen face drooped and her cloudy blue eyes stared off into space. The stroke forced one side of her mouth into a permanent frown.

"Hey, Mom," Crave's voice broke. "Do you remember me," he asked as he crouched down in front of her.

Crave took her thin hands into his, inwardly cringing at the soft, papery feel of them. He remembered a time when they were strong and bore slight callouses. Nettie seemed frailer than she had when he'd visited a few weeks ago.

She still didn't look at him.

"Nettie, I brought you a few things, some of those chocolates you like. The Lady saw me and instantly started putting your order together."

Crave released her hands and slipped off his backpack. He pulled out the bag of truffles, her favorite shampoo, and lotion.

"I'll go get the patio ready," he said as he reached out to gently squeeze her hand.

He straightened, then went to grab a basin, pitcher, and towel. She'd always loved her hair washed, he knew the nurses didn't have time to do more than simply get her clean and move on.

Once he had everything set out, he returned and took one of her hands, then slipped one around her back. She went where he led her and nothing more

He felt the hardness of bone. They'd told him a year ago, to prepare. Five years past since the last beating, he'd just pulled into Cozumel for a short stay. It had been his first vacation since he'd settled in Powers. He'd ignored the strange number for days before he finally answered. She'd lied to him during each phone call, and he'd let her, knowing it wasn't okay.

Crave had lost count of how many times he'd tried to convince her to leave. Promised her everything she'd ever want or need, and she'd refused. The way she was now as much his fault as the bastard who had beat her so badly she barely remembered her own name. Years of her life gone.

Crave shook his head and concentrated on Nettie. He settled her in the chair and gently picked apart her thick, silvery blonde braid.

And he talked. Eventually, she'd say something, but it always took a while.

"Twitch is still stealing my shirts. You remember the last one I wore here. He seems to like that one best."

He helped her tilt her head back and dampened her hair with warm water.

"I love him, Mom, and I fucked up, I almost hit him. I saw how scared he was."

He worked the shampoo into her hair.

"You'd love him too if you met him. He's beautiful. I didn't deserve him anyway."

He dropped his chin to his chest and tried to take a deep breath, but his lungs felt like they seized up.

"My Vinnie's gonna bring me home a son-in-law one day. He's handsome, are you a friend of his?" Her voice wobbled and slurred a bit as she spoke.

Crave bit his lip. He'd never told her he was gay, but she'd known. She confessed it was one of the reasons she'd made him promise to leave and never come back.

"Yeah, I'm a friend of his." Some visits she remembered who he was, but this didn't seem to be one of them. He went along with her just to be able to keep her with him a bit longer before she'd fade again.

"Does, does he have someone?"

"I think he used to, his name was Twitch."

"What was he like?"

"Absolutely gorgeous. Long dark hair. The most beautiful almond shaped green eyes. Petite. A temper when…Vinnie got too cocky."

"Did he take care of Vinnie?"

"Yes, he took great care of your son."

"Good, good, Vinnie needs someone to treat him nice. He ain't ever had that. Plus, he's a bit of a slob."

Crave laughed. "Tilt your head back so I can rinse your hair."

"Vinnie used to do this for me. Swear that boy brushed my hair for a good hour. Surprised I didn't go bald, but it made my baby happy. He needed to learn…"

"Learn what," Crave asked, he stripped the suds from her hair with gentle fingertips.

"To be gentle, a partner needs tenderness. Needs to be loved. He wasn't given the best example. I wish I hadn't made him promise to stay away. Do you think you can bring him to visit?"

"I'll see what I can do."

"What's your name," Nettie asked, she peered up at him.

He finished rinsing the last of the soap from her hair and wrung out the thick mass.

"My name is…Crave." He pretended because he didn't want to upset her.

"Weird name."

"Yeah, it is."

"Do you have someone, Crave?"

His mind instantly brought Twitch's image to the forefront. He'd loved the beautiful man forever, but terrified to admit it to himself. Guilt slowly ate away at him. What he'd allowed to happen to his mother. He knew he didn't deserve Twitch, but always too selfish to let the man go.

"I thought I did, but I fucked up."

"Did you hit them?"

"No, never, I'd…I was definitely short with him. I just wanted him safe."

"Men, they're all the same. You can't control everything, especially someone you want to make yours. You don't trap them, stifle them, because it only makes them want to run away."

"Did you ever want to run away?"

"So many times."

She lapsed into silence as the light in her eyes faded. The moments of conversation were brief. He spent an hour brushing her hair until it dried into a sleek fall around her shoulders, then braided it the way she always liked. Crave had to go home, back to the farm and Twitch. He knew it would only be to say goodbye and pack his things.

He helped Nettie inside and tucked her into bed, her lids were heavy. Crave straightened her covers, then leaned over and brushed a kiss across her forehead.

"I love you, Mom."

"I love you too, Vinnie."

He bit his lip to suppress a sob and lowered his forehead to her shoulder. His mother's breathing already evened out, and he listened to her delicate snores. Crave's shoulders shook as he let himself lose it. He needed to savor the moment because he didn't know when he'd hear his mother say his name and tell him she loved him again.

■■■■

Four hours later, he pulled to a stop beside the guys' motorcycles. It was Sunday, their regular night off. The house was unusually dark. Even when they didn't have to work everyone still stuck to their usual schedule. It was only a little past midnight. He dismounted and left his backpack in his saddlebags.

Crave didn't plan to stay long. Hell, he didn't know if he was welcome. First, he'd pack a bag and then search for Twitch and Bull. He quietly let himself inside and softly walked to his bedroom, the door was cracked.

He eased it open and froze at what he saw. Twitch laid in the middle of Crave's bed.

"He hasn't slept anywhere else." Bull's voice came from behind him. "You left him, Crave."

"I almost…"

"Fuck, man, you're a moron."

"I could've hurt him. You didn't see the look on his face."

"Did you hit him?"

"No, but—"

"There's no buts about it, Crave. You stopped that punch as soon as you saw it was Twitch. There's definitely no excuse for you leaving him. That fucker who Twitch took out nearly broke his jaw."

He jerked his gaze around to Twitch. Crave ignored the urge to rush to the bed and search Twitch for injuries.

"Is he, did someone take him out?"

"Scary and Tank took care of it, but that should have been you taking care of your fucking man. Not us, Crave, you."

"Did he go to the hospital?"

"Helluva bruise. A split lip. Nothing that won't heal. But you made him promise you something, and he didn't break it."

"What?"

"That he'd come only to you when he needed comfort and safety, affection. Priest and Lucky came out here, he sent them away. He hasn't slept in his own bed. He hasn't gone to work. Loving someone with Twitch's past is a huge responsibility, and that means you don't fucking run."

"I love him." Crave turned his body to lean against the door frame, but didn't take his eyes off Twitch. He took in the shallow indent of Twitch's spine. His lightly tanned skin flawless and looked silky. Two days away from Twitch was too long.

"You've got a shit way of showing it. You here to finally tell Twitch that you want him as yours or just to pack your shit?"

Crave almost lied, but decided against it, "I'd planned to pack."

"I thought you'd gave up running a decade ago."

"I'm no good for Twitch, what if I get angry and don't pull the next punch?"

"How many fucking times do I have to tell you, you're not your bastard of a dad before you fucking believe it?"

"I don't want to hurt him."

"That's the difference, man. Your old man didn't give a fuck about hurting you or your mother. What would you do if you left, found out Twitch found some man, then that man turned out to be like your father? How much guilt would you live with after that?

"Make this right, Crave. Your man has downed anxiety meds like candy, refuses even the most casual contact with me, Lucky, or Priest. The only person he's allowed near him is Lou, and that's only because he loves feeling his soon-to-be nephew move. He can't curl up to a Crave-sized body pillow for the rest of his life. Make it right, or I'll take your ass to the ring and then kick you the fuck off my property."

It was all Bull had said before he disappeared.

Crave stayed in the doorway. Twitch cuddled closer to the body pillow. Twitch's whimpering drew him away from the door, and he closed it as quietly as possible behind him. He toed off his boots, shucked his jeans, and reached back to grab his t-shirt between his shoulders tugging it over his head. Crave lifted the covers and laid down behind Twitch.

He sighed heavily as soft, warm skin pressed to his bigger, hairier body. It felt right, he knew he should get up and walk away. That would be the selfless thing to do; Twitch deserved a better man than him, but Crave couldn't let another man have Twitch. He loved the man too much.

Twitch turned over and nuzzled Crave's chest, small hands combed through the thick mat of hair. Twitch's contented sigh warmed his skin. Crave slid his left arm beneath Twitch's head and laid the other on the small man. A groan rumbled his chest as Twitch worked to get closer to him. Soft lips rubbed over his chest, up to his throat and his stubble-covered chin.

His cock hardened against Twitch's soft belly. He loved the softness of Twitch.

"You came home," Twitch sleepily whispered.

"I'm so sorry, baby, I'd never…"

Twitch's mouth pushed gently to his.

"Shh, I've never thought you would. I know why you ran, but don't do it again."

"I won't."

"Promise? Please."

Crave raised his hand to cup the side of Twitch's beautiful face and pressed his thumb beneath the cute, pointed chin. He looked down into Twitch's sleepy eyes with their long, thick lashes.

"I promise, and we'll talk when we wake up, okay?"

Twitch nodded, their lips rubbing together. "Did you go see your mom?"

"Yes."

"Is she okay?"

"As well as she can be, maybe you'd like to meet her."

"Really," Twitch asked as a wide smile tugged at the corners of his lush mouth.

"Yeah, maybe next Sunday. It's about a three-hour ride. Maybe I can take you to dinner." He tilted Twitch's head back farther. "You can get all prettied up for me."

"An actual date?"

"Yeah, one of those. Something I should've done a long time ago."

"We'll talk about it in the morning, I want to sleep. Our bed isn't the same without you."

"Our bed," Crave asked, he loved the sound of it.

"Yours is bigger and the mattress better than mine."

"Pain in my ass."

Twitch giggled, the sound soothing him as it always had. It was a happy sound, one he associated with the farm—with home.

"I'm sorry about this." He tenderly stroked the bruise on Twitch's cheek. "I should've been there."

"I've had worse. This wasn't your fault. I should've stayed behind the bar, but I couldn't let him hurt you."

"Hurt me," Crave asked.

"He came up behind you with a knife. I couldn't just…"

"My hero." He tried to joke even as the what ifs played in his head. He could've lost Twitch.

"Don't make fun and I already got yelled at."

"Not by me, but we'll wait, I have to think of a suitable punishment."

"Fine," Twitch sighed.

Twitch lowered his head to nuzzle his chest and Crave closed his eyes as he drew Twitch closer. Fuck being selfless, years he'd waited for him, and he wasn't giving him up. He just had to figure out how to be better; to be the partner Twitch needed. No matter what it took, he'd make Twitch happy.

16 IF HE WASN'T GOING TO DO IT, TWITCH DAMN WELL WOULD

Oh damn, he was so warm, Twitch snuggled deeper under the covers and closer to Crave's big body. Crave laid on his back, his hand over Twitch's thigh that somehow he'd thrown over Crave in the night. Twitch peeked from under the edge of the blanket and watched Crave sleep. The man was relaxed, he didn't wear his usual smirk or scowl and Crave looked almost adorable.

At that thought, Twitch snorted. He had a lot running through his head the last few days without Crave. Not once in all the years he'd known Crave, did the thought of the man physically hurting him pop into his head. And the other night at the bar hadn't changed that. He'd lost his head for a minute, he'd known better than to come up behind any of the guys during a brawl.

He also understood why Crave ran, but he couldn't have that happen again. Crave made him promise to always come to him, and Twitch wouldn't break it, but that meant

Crave needed to be there when Twitch needed him. Twitch drew his fingertips through the thick, dark golden hair on Crave's chest. He'd discovered he loved to touch Crave and have the big man touch him.

Touching in the recent past always meant comfort, but he wanted something else. Twitch knew Crave didn't push and wouldn't, so he'd made a decision. If Crave wasn't going to do it, he damn well would. For the moment of truth, could he break free of his anxiety and do what he needed without completely embarrassing himself?

Twitch eased the sheet and blanket off Crave and slowly shifted to his knees. He took a deep breath through his nose and exhaled as straddled Crave. He shook his head when he could barely touch the mattress with his knees.

Okay, that's a bit disconcerting, Twitch didn't know how he felt about the thick ridge of Crave's cock under his backside.

He placed his palms on the fuzzy, ridged plane of Crave's stomach. He kept his touch light, not yet wanting to wake Crave. Twitch froze as Crave arched up into the caress of his hands. Just a few more minutes, he didn't know what the hell he was doing. Yes, he knew the mechanics, but Crave's experience intimidated him.

Twitch bent over and laid his cheek on Crave's chest, listening to the steady rhythm. He placed his hands flat on the mattress and slid his body upward, his mouth hovered over Crave's full lips.

You can do this, Twitch! He mentally gave himself a pep talk. Who the hell had to talk themselves into kissing the man they loved? Apparently, him.

It wasn't going to work, he straightened and tried to force back his tears.

Crave needed someone normal, you didn't balk at a fucking kiss. He started to slide from atop Crave when the man's big hand caught him at the back of his neck and pulled him down. Soft, yet firm lips tenderly conformed to his, and he moaned. Crave was so much bigger than him yet he felt safe.

Crave lifted his head and Twitch slipped his arms around Crave's neck. He let Crave lead, and it seemed right, so very right.

He felt the deep rumble of Crave's growl against his mouth. Crave prodded the seam of Twitch's lips with the tip of his tongue. There wasn't any resistance, Twitch opened to let Crave inside.

The lingering kiss slowly ended and Crave started to pull back, but Twitch sucked on Crave's tongue earning another growl.

As Crave rocked him against the hardness of his stomach Twitch couldn't help the hard shiver down his spine. A pleasure he'd never dreamed of feeling pulled at his groin.

He was vaguely aware of Crave splaying his huge hand on his ass. Crave dug his fingers into Twitch's crease through the fabric of his pink briefs.

Twitch squeaked as Crave surged to a sitting position and ran his rough hands over every inch of Twitch he could reach.

He waited for the panic and shame, the need to escape. It didn't make an appearance, all he felt was the strangeness of desire and the need to get closer.

Twitch jerked his arms from around Crave's neck and pushed them between the tight press of their bodies until he reached his target. He nudged Crave's boxer briefs down and then wrapped his small hand around the thickness of Crave's dick.

"Fuck," Crave hissed through his clenched teeth.

Crave painfully flexed his fingertips into Twitch's hips. The big man fell backward and covered his face with his forearm.

Twitch looked down, he held his breath and part of his brain begun to analyze his reaction. His stomach fluttered with nerves. His balls ached, and his cock hardened. Every muscle in his body seized as a shudder worked through him. Crave's skin was silky and smooth in his hand, he stroked slowly and felt the jerk of Crave's cock against his palm.

Crave's large body arched and lifted Twitch, Twitch laid his free hand on Crave's stomach to brace himself.

A strange sense of power heated his body and made sweat bead on his skin. He released Crave's cock and listened to the deep growl in the man's chest. Twitch gently traced the veined, ruddy length and then along the ridge of the head. Pre-cum beaded at Crave's slit and pooled on the man's tanned belly just under his outie belly button.

He leaned forward and shivered as his soft stomach conformed to Crave's cock. He pushed Crave's arm aside and studied his strained features. Twitch flattened his hands on the bed above Crave's shoulders. He pushed upward, and his thighs squeezed Crave's sides as their dicks notched together. The only thing keeping them apart was Twitch's underwear.

He squealed as he suddenly found himself on his back with Crave beside him. Twitch felt the beginning of panic building steadily as Crave frantically jerked Twitch's underwear down his legs.

His eyes and mouth went wide as wet heat surrounded his dick, and his fingers grabbed Crave's hair. The backs of his thighs pushed against Crave's broad shoulders. Crave quickly bobbed along his dick. The tip of Crave's tongue working the underside. His toes curled as he sunk his heels into the muscles of Crave's back. His heart painfully beat against his ribs. The ceiling fan blew a cool breeze across his overheated, sweaty skin. Just as his sac tightened and he realized he was close to his first orgasm, Crave pulled away.

Twitch panicked and jerked hard at Crave's soft hair.

The bastard chuckled, then Crave's mouth was on his, and his tongue thrust past his lips. The kiss hard and dominating, then Twitch arched off the bed as rough fingertips massaged around his hole.

He squeezed his eyes closed as just the tip of one finger pushed inside. The kiss turned gentle and Crave whispered, whatever Crave said was lost in the roar of blood in his ears. He dug his fingers into the unrelenting muscles of Crave's biceps. Crave's touch disappeared for a minute and then cool, slick fingers returned to his hole.

"Twitch, baby, tell me you're ready," Crave ordered, one, then two fingers thrust inside Twitch.

He'd read enough to know he needed to push out and a shaky sigh pushed passed his lips.

"Open those pretty lips and tell me, I'll stop if—"

"If you stop," Twitch moaned, "I'll kill you."

How the hell had he went without this? Or was it because it was Crave, the man he loved?

It must've been all Crave needed because the man quickly stretched him. He lifted his hips, working himself onto Crave's fingers. He whimpered and protested as Crave disappeared, he opened his eyes to find Crave sitting back on his heels. His eyes widened as he watched Crave roll a condom down his flushed cock. Twitch darted a glance at Crave's face, red highlighted the man's cheeks, and the muscles in his neck strained. The man seemed larger and more dangerous, Twitch shook from head to toe.

"Turn over, hands and knees." Crave's voice was strained and gravelly.

His face flushed as he rolled over and embarrassment caused his dick to start to soften. He softly hissed as cold lube ran down his crease. He felt the heat of Crave blanketing his back.

"Just relax, baby, and push—"

A groan tickled the side of his neck as Crave pushed inside, the burn and pain caused him to try and pull away.

"Baby, easy."

He felt every inch of Crave's corded muscles trembling against his back and thighs.

Crave held still, Twitch realized the big man wasn't going to move until Twitch was ready. That alone had him relaxing, he squeezed around Crave's cock and listened to the man growl.

"You're fucking playing with fire."

He didn't know what came over him, he pushed back and felt the hot, glide of Crave's dick sinking deeper. He'd expected more pain, but only the burn intensified as well as the beginning of pleasure. He held his breath as he rocked back and forth, working Crave deeper.

Crave still hadn't moved just let him have control. Twitch dropped his forehead to the pillow and fisted his hands in the sheet until Crave bottomed out. He felt an overwhelming loss as Crave straightened, Crave's large hands gripped his hips.

"You ready, baby, I can't…" Crave growled.

Whatever control Crave held onto shattered as Crave took him in long, smooth thrusts. Crave grunted behind him, and he mirrored each one with a whimper, his ass felt on fire, but the pleasure quickly overrode the discomfort of moments before.

He turned his head to look back over his shoulder to take in the brutal beauty of Crave's hard, sweaty body, the deep concentration on his handsome face. His face flamed at the sight of Crave staring down.

"S'fucking sexy, stretch tight, fuck—"

Crave fell over him as Crave took his mouth in a commanding kiss. Crave increased the power of his thrusts, rocking Twitch's body and Twitch lost all control. He squealed, screamed and begged.

"Stroke yourself, I can't…"

Twitch momentarily hesitated before he grabbed his cock and stroked in a frantic pace as his body strained toward his first release. He'd dreamed of this moment, Crave was the only one he'd ever thought about taking him—loving him.

His cock ached as he faintly heard the dirty things Crave whispered in his ear. While it should've embarrassed him, it only made him want more. His mouth fell open as he screamed, cum spilled over his fingers and Crave took him faster and harder. The sounds of sweaty skin slapping and Crave's cock thickened, teeth sunk into his shoulder as Crave's last thrust forced Twitch's body in a deep arch.

The pleasure was too much, and his eyes rolled upward under his closed lids. Muscles he didn't even know he had shook before he collapsed, Crave came with him. The big man instantly tried to roll away, but Twitch reached back to wrap his hands around Crave's nape.

He tried to process, the wet spot under him cooling and uncomfortable, but the press and weight of Crave on top of him perfect. He could really get used to that.

"Baby, you okay." Crave's voice was broken and raspy.

Twitch didn't trust his own voice, so he just nodded. He was all right, but his brain was starting to over analyze, and he shut it down. Twitch wasn't ready to think, there would be plenty of time later—much later.

17 THIS DATING THING WASN'T
SO HARD

Crave tried not to grin too widely at Twitch bouncing on his toes outside Nettie's room. Twitch had practically vibrated since they'd left the house. The door opened, and Twitch jumped, a pleasant-faced nurse walked out.

"Hey, Vincent, your mother will be so happy to see you. She's having an excellent day."

"Thanks, Vera, this is Twitch, I brought him to meet Mom."

"Hi, Twitch, pleased to meet you. Vincent hasn't brought a guest before."

"I'm so excited to meet her." Twitch's nervousness sent his voice up a few octaves.

Crave couldn't take his gaze away from Twitch even as he listened to Vera laugh. He'd been terrified about bringing Twitch there. It was hard enough dealing with Nettie not knowing who he was; he didn't know how he'd handle it with a witness especially when it was Twitch.

The small man was too excited about meeting her for Crave to even think of changing his mind. Besides he wanted Nettie to meet the man he loved, even if she didn't remember Crave.

"Come on, you're gonna give yourself a heart attack," Crave said with a laugh as he pushed the door open, ushering Twitch inside with his hand splayed across Twitch's lower back.

"Oh my God," Twitch whispered.

Crave braced himself. Her hair wasn't done the way she liked. He knew the way she was before. Remembered how beautiful she'd been and Twitch only saw the present version. Maybe this hadn't been...

"She's a beautiful female version of you. Now, introduce me all proper."

Twitch slipped his arm through his and tugged him forward.

"Hi, Mom." He leaned down to kiss her cheek. "I brought someone to meet you."

She lifted her head and smiled, Crave felt the tears yet pushed them back.

"Vinnie, you came home, is it." She paused as panic filled her cloudy, blue eyes.

He released Twitch and fell to his knees to take her hands. "It's okay, he's gone, it's just the two of us, remember? You're safe, I promise."

Out of everything she could remember, not him but the terror of her ex-husband's abuse. He lifted her hands to his mouth and brushed kisses across her knuckles.

"Hi, I'm Twitch."

He turned his head to find Twitch kneeling beside him. His long hair shielding his face as Twitch dug through his bag.

"Are you Vinnie's?"

Crave frowned as Twitch flinched. After the other day did Twitch not think he didn't belong to Crave?

"Yes, he's mine, I've told you about him."

"He's beautiful, son, you did good."

As Nettie raised her hand to rub Crave's cheek, the corners of his mouth pulled into a broad smile. He lifted his own to hold her cool hand to his skin.

"I think so too."

Maybe they should've had that talk before the sex. He'd semi-lost his head when he'd awakened to find Twitch straddling him. Twitch gifted him with his first time and what had he done: taken without saying he loved Twitch. Shit, one more fuck up to atone for, great.

"Cr...Vinnie says he knows how you like your hair, but he sucks at doing nails. Princess asked him once..."

Crave sat down on the floor to watch and listen to Nettie and Twitch. Twitch expertly cut, filed, and began to paint her nails all the while keeping up a steady stream of conversation. He didn't think he could fall harder for the small man, but the more Nettie smiled and laughed, the more he loved him.

It was the longest Nettie stayed in the present in years. He reached out to tuck Twitch's hair behind the perfect whorl of his ear, then stroked gently across his cheek.

Twitch flashed him a shy smile and went back to painting delicate flowers on Nettie's nails. Crave didn't have an idea of all the tools Twitch had pulled from his bag, but whatever they were Twitch knew how to use them.

The small man had a lot of hidden talents.

"I like your makeup," Nettie wistfully whispered.

"Good, because I brought you a few things. Vinnie said he'd take care of your hair and then I'll finish making you even more beautiful."

He raised his hand to scrub his palm over his face, and then rested his chin on it. Nettie's pale cheeks flushed at the compliment.

They spent the afternoon with Nettie, Twitch pampering her, but slowly he noticed her tiring, her memory fading. Crave held onto Nettie's hand, and then he helped her to bed. He tucked the covers around her. He tensed as Twitch's hand rubbed up and down his back.

"I'm sorry, I didn't…"

"Why are you apologizing? We had a great day with your mom. Nothing better than that."

He straightened and slipped his arm around Twitch. "I wanted her to last a bit longer."

"Did you ever think of moving her closer to home?"

"I thought about moving her in with me, but I don't have my own place, our hours are turned the fuck around."

He leaned down and kissed Twitch's soft hair. It wasn't like he'd never thought about getting a place of his own and hire a nurse to come in, but he lived cheaply so he could afford the best for his mom. Crave turned his attention back to his mom and watched her as she slept.

"Couldn't we bring her to the farm? Bull can't tell me no," Twitch said sweetly.

"Manipulative."

"I have my moments."

"Ready to go have dinner, we were here longer than I'd planned."

"That was awesome. I loved meeting her, maybe next time we can take her to dinner with us."

"We'll see if she's having a good day next time."

He leaned down to kiss Nettie's cheek and to softly tell her goodbye. He led Twitch from the room and then outside.

"We have to talk." He set sideways on his bike to put himself eye level with Twitch.

"Aw, man, come on, you promised me a greasy burger and fries, and ice cream," Twitch whined.

"I'm still going to get you ice cream, but, Twitch, when Mom asked were you mine, you didn't say shit."

"I didn't know what to say."

"Why?"

"We never talked about it. I didn't want to assume..."

"You're mine. Always have been. Do you know how many fuckers I threatened who even smiled at you?"

Twitch pushed his chest. "Is that why you got into so many fights?"

"Damn right, baby, someone else taking you home wasn't fucking happening." He reached out to grab Twitch's hips and pull the smaller man between his thighs. "I've spent so many years thinking I was just like him. No fucking way was I taking the chance that...then the other night I almost hit you."

Twitch lifted onto his toes and pushed his soft lips to his, Crave took advantage and kissed Twitch liked he'd wanted to do for days. He grumbled as Twitch pulled back and rubbed his small hands over his chest. His cock jerked at even the most innocent touch from his little man.

"You're not him, Crave, and that night I wasn't afraid of you. I knew better than to come up behind one of y'all, especially you during a fight. I got stupid, and I learned from my mistake. Next time someone tries to knife you in the back you're on your own."

"I can feel the fucking love, baby."

"So, does this mean you're my boyfriend? Going all steady and shit?"

"Your first and your last."

"Crave, don't…"

"I'm making the promise. Like I said you're mine and if I'm lucky enough you'll spend every night in my bed. I let you keep your distance since, but that's over."

"I didn't want to crowd you."

"You could never crowd me." Crave bit back confessing his love.

Twitch still wasn't sure of him, and that hurt, but Crave knew he had a lot to prove to Twitch first. He had to make sure Twitch knew how serious he was and Crave wanted forever, a wedding band or inked ring. He didn't care which as long as Twitch knew he only belonged to Crave.

"So, you gonna take me on our first official date?"

"Whatever you want."

"Now, now, Crave, don't tempt me, whatever I want leaves a lot of options," Twitch said, his lashes fluttering.

"Flirt."

Crave nudged Twitch back, mounted his bike and patted the spot behind him. Twitch gracefully climbed up behind him.

"I still think Mom should come home with us," Twitch said, then went silent.

Crave glanced over his shoulder to find Twitch putting on his helmet. He already saw that becoming a frequent conversation. Facing forward he put on his own helmet unable to keep the smile off his face. Soon, he'd show and tell Twitch how much he loved him, first, he needed to make it through their first date.

18 SHIT, THIS WASN'T HOW HE WANTED TO START HIS DAY

Twitch stretched and tried to roll to his stomach, but the steely band of Crave's muscled arm kept him pressed to the sturdy length of the big man's body. He contentedly sighed as he savored the warmth. His eyes opened, and he glanced at the clock on the bedside table and groaned, eleven in the morning. That was practically obscene, who the hell woke up that early?

A week passed since Crave and him had sex, he was starting to wonder if they man still wanted him. Crave didn't push, he'd even gotten advice from Landon, Lucky and Priest. He'd given clues, tried to take their kisses and make out sessions further, but Crave was still being so good. Twitch didn't like it, and he was getting desperate.

"Whoever the fuck is knocking on my door, better fucking be dying," Bull's voice boomed through the house.

"Oh shit." Twitch struggled from the bed, dressed quickly in one of Crave's t-shirts and Twitch's favorite hot pink, leopard print pajama bottoms.

Bull wasn't friendly on a good day, awake before noon and the man turned homicidal. He threw open the door and found Bull standing in the open doorway, shirtless, and his jeans hung low on his hips. Of course Bull would practically be cock out to answer the door.

"Twitch, it's for you, tell them not to fucking show up before goddamned noon…" Bull spun from the door.

Once the big man was out of the way, Twitch found his parents standing on the porch. His dad was in his usual conservative suit, his dark brown hair perfectly style, and a disapproving expression on his handsome face.

His mother stood slightly behind, her silky, black hair twisted up into an elegant chignon. Her petite frame wearing a designer dress, the classic little black dress. She was petite, perfect, and beautiful.

Twitch took after her more than his father.

"Mother, Father, this is…a surprise. I wasn't aware you were coming for a visit."

That's because they'd never once come to his home before. He'd always been summoned to their place. Twitch nervously shifted as he became aware of them taking in his outfit. He knew his curly hair was wild and a bit tangled. He smoothed Crave's shirt trying to get rid of the wrinkles and instantly became mad at himself.

"Evan, we came to visit your Grandmother, she told us your…address."

Weston's nose snarled with disgust as he looked around the house. He took pride in his home. Twitch ran the place smoothly and kept four growly men in line on a daily basis. He had nothing to be ashamed of, and he wouldn't let his father make him embarrassed.

"Please, come in, I'll make some coffee." Twitch stepped forward and motioned them inside.

"Baby, why are you up, come back to bed," Crave's sleep-roughened voice barely sounded before his arms were around Twitch, attempting to pull him back into the bedroom.

"Crave, my parents are here."

"Oh, yeah, what do they…"

Crave seemed to catch himself.

"Maybe I should put on pants."

Twitch bit his lips and rolled them between his teeth to hide his amusement, but failed. "Probably best." He sensed when Crave disappeared back into the bedroom.

"Make me food," Psycho order seconds before he snatched Twitch off his feet.

He was placed like a kid on Psycho's hip. His ass braced on Psycho's arm as he was rushed to the kitchen.

Twitch could so die of mortification right about then. He glanced back to find his parents staring with their general disapproval when it came to him.

"Fuck, Psycho, put my man down," Crave ordered as he pushed passed Twitch's parents.

"You stole him last night, and I didn't get my food, this is becoming a habit, and I don't like it. This sharing shit sucks."

"Put me down." Twitch wiggled to get the huge man to let him go. "Psy, I made you food and left it in the fridge."

"Not the same."

Psycho would deny it to his dying day, but, damn, the man was cute as fuck when he pouted. Almost seven-feet of dangerous man shouldn't in any situation be considered cute, but, dammit, if he wasn't. Okay, not the appropriate time. His parents stared at him, and he could imagine what they thought. Bad enough they looked down on him because he lived with the guys, but now it looked like he had a houseful of boyfriends. He shook his head and forced away his smile.

"Psycho, my parents are here," he whispered in Psycho's ear.

"Can I kill them?"

"No, you can't."

"Dammit," Psycho growled then set Twitch carefully on his feet.

"Thank you."

"Don't thank me, I make no guarantees."

"Eight egg, veggie omelet?"

"I feel warm and fuzzy toward you."

That's as close as Psycho would ever get to saying the L-word. "I love you too." He turned to his parents, "Um, Psycho, Crave, and Bull, these are my parents, Weston and Caroline Harrison."

He cast his gaze around the kitchen, Bull was staring over the rim of his mug, still shirtless, and glared at Twitch's parents. He'd told Bull everything about growing up, and he knew Bull's opinion of the Harrison's. Bull glanced at him, and he silently implored the older man to behave and be nice.

"Twitch is making breakfast, you joining us?"

"No, we're not going to be here long, we'd like to speak with Evan in private."

"Baby," Crave whispered his name.

Crave's strong arms circled his waist and pulled him back against him.

"It's fine." He turned and lifted onto his toes to kiss Crave, a throat clearing behind him stopped him.

He stopped, then flinched as hurt moved through Crave's blue eyes. Twitch sensed the moment Crave began to pull away both emotionally and physically. He couldn't have that, Crave became his anchor, and the one person he didn't have to disguise all his crazy shit. Twitch raised his hands and grabbed Crave's face and tugged until his lips touched Crave's mouth.

"I'm sorry," he said, his lips trembled. He knew Crave probably wouldn't ever be over the belief he would end up like his abusive dad and in no way did Twitch want to make that worse.

"It's okay."

Crave's mouth tilted into a small smile and Twitch kissed him gently. His man tenderly stroked his back, and then he stepped away.

"You need me, I'll be in our room."

He couldn't suppress his smile at Crave calling his room their room. Twitch nervously wrung his hands as he helplessly watched as all the guys left the room leaving him alone with his parents. He barely restrained the urge to stroke his fingertips along with scars on his left side. Instead, he moved his right hand behind him. He tapped each finger to his thumb, index to pinkie, then reversed the order; he counted each touch.

"Would you like tea or coffee, I think I have some tea…"

"I believe we told that man we wouldn't be here long." His dad's cold voice cut right through him.

"Yes, I apologize."

"We've decided it's time for you to end this inappropriate behavior of yours. I've allowed it far too long."

"Inappropriate." He swallowed around the knot in his throat. "This is my home. The guys need me."

Twitch braced himself for the recitation of Scripture. The accusation of his supposed sins for giving into his deviant urges. Celibacy was the only way to save his soul from damnation.

"We'll reinstate your credit cards, rent you a suitable apartment, and unfreeze your trust fund."

They watched him with disappointment clear in their gazes, but worse than that was the disgust that existed there too. He was their only child, weren't they supposed to love him unconditionally?

"And what would I have to do," Twitch asked.

He'd lived by their rules for almost twenty-one years. Substituted the pleasure and love he'd never thought he'd have or deserve with pain and anxiety. They wanted him to go back to the before. Denying who he was and pretending—pretending happiness to appease them.

"Abstain as you did before. Repent—"

"Aw fuck no," Bull's deep growl echoed before his big body stepped up next to his.

Twitch acted without thought and wrapped his arms around Bull's waist, he ruffled the thick hair on Bull's stomach. He soaked in the warmth and comfort.

"Crave," Twitch whispered against Bull's skin.

"Right here, baby." Crave's strong hands extricated him from Bull. "Come here, let Bull handle this."

"Let me handle it," Psycho growled.

"Don't let Psy go to jail." That earned him a chuckle from the guys and an eye roll from Psycho.

"They won't let Psycho go to jail."

"Now," Bull spoke up, his voice too quiet, "This is what's going to happen. This is Twitch's home, and none of us invited you or your bullshit religion into our house."

Twitch grimaced as his dad started to open his mouth.

"If even one line of Scripture leaves your mouth, I'll take you down or let Psycho do it. Your fake God and Jesus represents love and acceptance, none of which calls for telling an innocent child he's going to Hell for being himself.

"You sent your fucking son to be tortured in conversion therapy to the point he's attempted killing himself. For that alone, I should knock your fucking teeth out."

"Bull…"

He didn't want Bull getting in trouble because of him. They weren't worth it.

"Twitch, I've watched you come home from visits, downing your fucking meds like candy. I'm done holding my tongue."

"Our son is our concern, this is a mockery in the face of God. Having relations with you all…"

The corners of his mouth jerked as the room erupted into gruff laughter. Crave shook against his side, even as he drew soothing circles at the small of his back.

"Really, that's how low, no, no, if he were in a relationship…"

Crave growled.

"Put it away, Crave, shit, you know he's yours, fuck, put a ring on his finger if you're so worried about someone taking him."

Psycho snorted. "I'll fight you for him, I'm still waiting for my damn omelet, I think I've lost fifty pounds since he hooked up with your fucking ass."

Twitch dared a look at his parents, disgust, and horror pinched their features deepening the lines around their mouths. All Twitch had ever wanted was his parents to love him. They didn't have to accept he was gay; didn't need to approve of it, just love him.

The small sliver of hope he'd held onto quickly died witnessing the revulsion of his family. The Brawlers and Twirled Crew were exactly that—his family. They'd accepted him without a second thought, annoying habits and all.

He'd attempted to live up to their expectations, attended counseling appointments, and smiled through the torture of so-called therapy. Twitch had tried, but he'd failed. At least that's what he'd thought, seeing the people who were his parents in his home, with the guys proved nothing he'd do would give Twitch real parents. Twitch turned to lean against Crave's side, but Crave's tattoo caught his attention, and he looked closer.

He traced the beautiful lines of Trouble's work, the delicate details of feathered wings, arched spine and the beautiful fall of dark curls. Crave's muscles danced beneath his touch.

"Is that me," Twitch asked, quickly glancing up, then back at the tattoo.

"Yes."

"Why, you got it before we…" He tried but failed not to peek at his parents.

Rough fingertips touched his cheek and brought his full attention back to Crave. Crave wore a soft, almost loving smile, no not loving, they'd never talked about that.

The bigger man slowly lowered until Crave's mouth tenderly brushed his.

"Let's go to our room and talk, okay?"

"Okay."

"Tell them goodbye, baby."

Twitch nodded, turned, and stepped up beside Bull. He took a deep, calming breath, and briefly analyzed the tangled, swirling thoughts in his head. They'd never love or accept him, no matter what he does it wouldn't matter.

"Don't come to my home again. This is my family now. You're not welcome." He sounded stronger than he felt. He pretended to be brave, a role he'd gotten far too good at playing, but he'd done it. As much as it hurt, these two people weren't welcome in his life, and he hoped one day they'd regret it more than him.

"Go on, son, we'll take out the trash."

"Thank you, Bull."

Bull didn't answer, simply put an arm around him, and Twitch inhaled the spicy scent of his skin. The older man's firm lips pressed to the top of his head. Twitch snorted at the growl behind him.

"Don't make me take your possessive ass to the ring," Bull threatened.

Twitch gave Bull a quick, tight hug before he spun back to Crave. He giggled as Crave threw him over his shoulder and stomped from the room.

"What about my goddamned omelet, bring him back here," Psycho bellowed.

"Sorry," he yelled as Crave slammed the door and locked them inside.

Twitch found himself set back on his feet so quickly it made him dizzy. Crave took his hands and tugged him forward until Crave took a seat on the end of the unmade bed. One hard jerk and he was plastered to Crave and nestled between his massive, muscled thighs.

"You wanted to ask me something?"

He laid his hand over Crave's tattoo and nervously nibbled on his bottom lip. Since they were alone, he wasn't so sure of himself. The sharp prod of his usual anxiety pushed in at the base of his skull and caused his skin to feel too tight and foreign. What if he asked a stupid question and Crave laughed or worse, looked at him with pity?

Crave rumbled, and the deep growl soothed him.

"No second thoughts, ask," Crave demanded, his strong hands squeezing Twitch's hips.

"Why?"

"You're mine. Have been since the minute you walked that sexy ass into Brawlers. You know why I kept it to myself, I still ain't all that sure of myself."

"Crave, you're not him. If you were, you wouldn't be as gentle as you are with your mom or even me. You wouldn't care if I was grounded or happy."

"I get that shit, my brain…" Crave shook his head, "I don't want to wake up one day and be him."

He took Crave's face in his hands and tilted the man's head up. Crave's hands absently rubbed along the sides of his thighs.

"I'll kick your ass if you do." He tried to keep what he hoped was a stern, don't fuck with me look on his face but rolled his lips between his teeth to suppress his smile.

"You're cute when you try to be badass."

"Hey, I'm tougher than I look, look at these." He leaned back to hold up his small fists.

Crave barked out laughter and Twitch pushed against his powerful chest, the big man fell backward.

"You're an asshole." His growl came out more like a purr, and that only set Crave off more. He jumped onto Crave and straddled the big man's hips. "And to think I loved your oversized, arrogant ass."

He realized what he'd said and froze at the same time as Crave. One minute he was sitting up and the next Crave rolled him beneath his big body.

"Say it again, and try it not in the past tense."

"Why?"

"Don't try the why shit with me, fucking say it."

"Maybe I don't wanna."

"Too damn bad, I love you too, and I want you to say it like you fucking mean it, please."

There was that fucking please again. "Will it get me more sex?" He loved the arrogant fucker, but he wasn't going to make it easy on Crave.

"Say it, and we'll see."

"I love you."

The words were barely out his mouth before Crave's mouth was on his, and his clothes disappeared. Oh yes, definitely more sex. He could deal with that.

19 OH FUCK, CRAVE COULD GET USED TO THIS

Crave laughed from his perch on the counter and watched a blushing and mortified Twitch doing everything within his power to ignore them. Okay, at the time Bull busted into their room, knocking the door off its hinges, ready to defend a screaming Twitch's honor wasn't funny, but now, the look on Bull and Twitch's faces were too much.

He wouldn't deny he was feeling a bit smug. Twitch responsiveness to his every touch and kiss, and to know it was only for him fed his already dangerous possessiveness toward the small man. He tried to pull back, curb it, but he'd waited years for Twitch to be his.

Bull was always grumpy, so the death glare wasn't unusual, but Twitch, he didn't like seeing his man embarrassed. He'd make it up to Twitch later with a ride and dinner.

Bull was the first to break the afternoon silence, "Twitch said you're moving your mom to town."

"I said we'd talk about it." He'd love to have Nettie closer, but there was a lot to plan for. She needed around the clock care.

"You know Harper from the bookstore," Twitch asked.

"Yeah."

"She has nursing experience and needs to make some extra money, she'd be willing to take care of Nettie on the weekends and a few mornings a week."

"She would huh?"

"Yes, and I looked at a small cottage style house a few streets over from Scary. Here I took pictures."

Crave leaned back as Twitch approached with his phone and settled between his legs. He took Twitch's phone and scrolled through at least a dozen pictures of the house.

Twitch practically vibrated and his smile bright, he loved Twitch even more right then. The man's slender hands absently stroked Crave's thighs, Crave raised his hand and wrapped it around Twitch's nape. He massaged Twitch's muscles until the small man somewhat calmed. Crave sensed his man was letting his nerves and anxiety take over. That wasn't what he wanted, he needed Twitch comfortable enough to be open and honest at all times.

Twitch sighed and smiled. "The rent is cheaper than what you pay a month to keep her at the other place. Her benefits and if we can add her to our insurance from work, it would cover a part-time live-in nurse, and we can spend our days off with her. This would be the best option, I thought about moving a trailer out here, but her living closer to town seemed safer since we're asleep half the day and gone most of the night.

"Don't say no, please, just think about it." Twitch's gaze implored him to consider it.

It amazed him the amount of time and thought Twitch had put into moving his mom closer to them.

"Harper already works full-time at Nightingale's."

"She's been crashing in Kyle's guest room, but she wants a place of her own, and with Kyle being a newlywed she feels bad."

"We'll have to talk to her—"

"Dr. Snyder said that—"

"When did you talk to her doctor?"

"When I went to visit Tuesday on my day off. We had lunch. I did her nails, and we went for a nice walk."

"I thought you went grocery shopping."

"I did after I left her so she could take her nap. She even stayed aware for two hours before she got tired. Nettie has a beautiful laugh, and I know where you got your twisted sense of humor."

Twitch stared up at him, his beautiful eyes shimmering with happiness. He tightened his hand, flexed and pulled Twitch to him. He crushed Twitch's mouth beneath his, ignoring the groans and grumbling around them. Crave's focus was entirely on Twitch.

Fuck, he could easily get used to this, Twitch was it, and he'd never been surer than right then. He slowly pulled back, reluctantly breaking the kiss, and bumped Twitch's cute tilted-tip nose with his.

"Love you," he whispered.

Twitch's lids fell as his face turned the prettiest shade of pink.

"Love you too."

"Want to go for a swim?"

"When?"

"Now."

"I'll be ready in fifteen, pack a picnic."

Twitch gave him one last kiss and took off running from the room.

"Love," Hunter's voice broke on a snort.

"Shut the fuck up, don't get jealous I got him."

Crave grinned as Hunter rolled his eyes and pushed his fingers through his loose hair.

"Don't fuck Twitch over because you just want a piece of ass."

He did a double take at the menace in the usually calm man's voice. Crave figured Hunter for a pacifist, he hadn't stepped into the Brawler's ring in the months he'd lived there. The younger man was more useless in a fight than Twitch, but something in Hunter's tone made Crave believe he'd better watch his step.

Then he looked at Psycho and Bull to find them wearing the same expression. Did they really think he only wanted Twitch for some fun and nothing else? He'd kept himself in check for four fucking years because he knew he wasn't good enough, hell, he knew his friends thought he wasn't either, but he was trying.

"Don't get your fucking manties in a bunch, Twitch just ain't exactly your usual type, and now you're talking love and shit." Psycho rolled his eyes.

"I do love him." And he did. Maybe always had and he refused the fuck it up. No matter what the guys thought of him, he was in it for the long run.

"We don't doubt it, we're just protective as fuck of Twitch. Shit ain't exactly been easy for him. I just want that boy happy." Bull turned to pour another mug of coffee.

"Better make your boy that picnic or he's gonna leave your fucking ass behind," Psycho griped. "Have him home for dinner, I'm tired of this fucking sharing bullshit. I should have got him first."

"You're obsessed with your goddamned stomach. Did you fall below 300?"

"I can feel my ribs," Psycho growled.

Crave laughed and shook his head as he jumped down from the counter. He quickly started to throw together some food, then made plans. An overnight camping trip. It would be nice to have Twitch all to himself for a night without overprotective friends who busted down doors and questioned his intentions. He knew what he wanted, and that was eventually a ring on Twitch's finger, he just needed to be patient a little longer.

■■■■

Crave leaned back in a camp chair with Twitch cradled on his lap. The small campfire kept the night chill away. They'd had to hike in since Bull's truck wouldn't make the trail. Twitch's head rested on his shoulder, his man's slender fingers laced with his, and he liked the comfortable quiet between them.

Twitch's soft tone broke the silence, "Do you ever think about having kids?"

"No." He grimaced at the harshness of his answer. "I love Princess and Juvie, but I've never really seen myself as a dad for obvious reasons. What about you?"

"No, not really, I think I thought about it a lot when my parents were trying to find me a suitable wife."

"That still trips me the fuck out." He turned his head to nuzzle Twitch's throat. "I can't imagine never knowing you."

"Through the torture and so-called therapy, I wished I was normal. I was never really interested in college, it turned into a way to escape, to maybe be me. It didn't work out that way."

"I'm gonna sound like the asshole I am, but I'm glad I got you first, and no one else touched what's mine."

"Your caveman tendencies are on fucking point."

"Sorry." He playfully grunted when a pointy elbow landed against his ribs.

"No, you're not."

"Okay, I'm not." Crave slipped his fingers from between Twitch's and slid his hands beneath Twitch's sweatshirt, well, another one Twitch had stolen from him. He smoothed his palms over the softness of Twitch's stomach and pushed his fingertips into the slight give. "You know why I brought you out here right?"

"To swim." Twitch breathing hitched.

He loved that little sound, and he strummed his thumbs across the hardness of Twitch's nipples and the barbells through them. Twitch arched, his rounded ass rubbed against Crave's hardening dick. He growled as he sucked at Twitch's quickening pulse.

"Want to try that again?"

"I can't help I'm a scre…"

A hard shudder went the full length of Twitch's small body.

"Don't fucking apologize for that. I love when you scream and beg for me to fuck you harder. Stand up," he ordered.

Even as Twitch obeyed, Crave reluctantly released him. He missed the silkiness and warmth of his skin, his slight weight. Twitch's nervousness was almost palatable as the small man stood before him.

"Strip." Crave unzipped his hoodie and removed it to throw it to the ground beside the chair. He spread his thighs to alleviate the pinch of denim on his cock. He licked his lips, tracking Twitch's every movement, and held his breath as Twitch reached for the bottom of the sweatshirt to slowly strip it away.

Twitch hesitated as he dropped it beside his small bare feet. He loved Twitch's shyness; the color in Twitch's cheeks he could barely see by firelight. Okay, he owned his asshole, Neanderthal tendencies when he came to his innocent man, but he loved everything about Twitch from his beautiful hair, even the scars that showed Twitch was a survivor, down to his cute toes with their pink polished nails.

He went against his natural bossiness and let Twitch strip at his own pace. Crave gripped the rounded ends of the armrests as he waited impatiently, then his reward was revealed in sexily slow increments. Flames and moonlight highlighted the perfect lines of Twitch's body.

Crave reached for the button of his jeans, he quickly released the painful pressure on his erection.

Twitch moaned, "Aren't you going to..." Twitch nibbled on the lower lip, "Strip."

Crave raised his arms to fist his t-shirt and tugged it over his head. As the cotton disappeared, he rumbled to find Twitch completely naked for him. He leaned forward and reached out to grab Twitch's trim hips, tugged him forward. Without warning, he swallowed Twitch's slender dick.

He groaned at Twitch's taste and the sweet, muskiness of his scent. Twitch always smelled like vanilla and lemon. His lover's slim fingers combed through his hair. Twitch's short nails scored his scalp, and Crave smoothed his hands around to grip the two perfect curves of Twitch's ass. He licked and sucked, bobbed along Twitch's length until Twitch started to thrust between his lips.

Twitch whimpered and trembled, and Crave needed more. His fingertips skimmed Twitch's silky skin. The fine hairs on Twitch's thighs tickled his palms. He jerked one of his hands away from Twitch and reached down to release his cock. Crave shuddered at the pleasure.

Twitch leaned forward, his back bowed as his chest rested on Crave's head. He tightly hugged Twitch's thighs as he withdrew, Twitch's cock slipped from between his lips. He reclined and tilted his head until he could take the smaller man's mouth. He lost all control as he roughly kissed Twitch; he stroked every inch of Twitch he could reach.

The night air cooled his sweaty skin and Twitch shuddered against him. He surged to his feet, lifted Twitch into his arms, and headed for their tent without breaking the kiss.

He never thought much about kissing, but with Twitch it turned out to be his favorite thing. Being Twitch's first in everything still humbled him, and he wanted to make sure Twitch never regretted it.

He dropped to his knees and knee walked into the tent, he absently struggled the zipper closed. He laid Twitch on the air mattress they'd made earlier. Crave turned on the camp lantern and knelt there studying every inch of Twitch splayed out before him like an offering. He noticed something different, Twitch didn't attempt to conceal his scars when the light came on. Crave knew his little man still bore a bit of self-consciousness and shame for them.

"Do you know how fucking beautiful you are," Crave asked, he placed his hands on Twitch's ankles, curled his hands and stroked upward.

As he reached Twitch's soft inner thighs and his thumbs kneaded the backs, pushed them open wide. The position exposed the tight, little hole and he moved his hands until he massaged Twitch's opening.

"Not beaut…" The word broke on a gasp.

Crave lowered, pushed his face between Twitch's cheeks and tongued the wrinkled skin. The muscles flexed and eased, he fucked Twitch with the tip of his tongue. Twitch's thighs shook, and he tried to close them, Crave forced them back to Twitch's chest.

Twitch's sexy, little whimpers, his scent, and taste overwhelmed him. He'd quickly became addicted to it all; he wanted Twitch even more than he did before. That should've been damn near impossible.

He licked upward, sucked at Twitch's balls, and then traced the length of Twitch's cock, enjoyed the flex of it under his tongue. Crave kissed every inch of Twitch's stomach and chest, paying extra attention to Twitch's scars. He canted his gaze to watch Twitch. His man's eyes were closed, his mouth open as he panted, and Twitch arched.

Crave's knees sunk in the mattress as he knelt between Twitch's slender thighs.

"Open your eyes, baby," he huskily whispered as he sucked at Twitch's pounding pulse. He rested his weight on his hands and knees, hovering over Twitch.

Twitch's lashes fluttered, then opened his eyes, and Twitch's lids were heavy.

He lowered to his forearms, bracketed Twitch's beautiful face in his hands, and stroked his thumbs across Twitch's high cheekbones. Twitch was so delicate compared to him.

"Do you even understand how lucky I feel? To be able to touch you, tell everyone you're fucking mine," he growled, bumped the point of Twitch's chin with his nose, then kissed the corners of his man's full, plump mouth. "The moment I fucking saw you." He kissed Twitch's bottom lip. "I wanted you. Every time someone flirted, tried to take you home, was hell. Knowing—" Crave laid his forehead on Twitch's.

Twitch softly called his name.

"It killed me when you brought men to the house."

"I felt guilty as fuck, I'm sorry."

Twitch tenderly combed his fingers through his hair and Crave closed his eyes, then slowly opened them. How the fuck did he get so lucky?

"Don't be, being with me wouldn't have been fair…"

"Shut up, you're just what I want, always needed."

He kissed Twitch long and deep, Twitch's tongue dancing over his, and Crave pulled away. He straightened to sit back on his heels, he thrust his hand into his backpack, pulled out a condom and a small bottle of lube.

Quickly as possible, he stretched Twitch until his man was fucking himself onto three of Crave's fingers. He couldn't wait any longer, he slipped his fingers from Twitch, quickly rolled on the condom, slicked up his covered cock. Crave's chest rose with his quickened breaths. The night air cooled the sweat on his back as he gripped the base of his dick, pressed the fat head to Twitch's stretched hole and pushed until he popped inside. He entered Twitch in one smooth glide until he was balls deep. His muscles tightened and strained as he blanketed Twitch's smaller frame.

He whispered encouragement as he began a slow pace, his movements quickened with the increasing crescendo of Twitch's whimpers and moans. Crave alternated between dirty and sweet talk. Twitch's short nails scored his back. His heels dug into Crave's ass.

A high-pitched squeak told him he'd found Twitch's prostate and Crave aimed for it repeatedly until Twitch begged for faster and harder. His muscled stomach rubbed Twitch's hard cock, pre-cum joining the sweat on Crave's hairy belly.

"Fuck, baby, cum for me," Crave ordered against Twitch's mouth.

Twitch's small, slim body tightened and arched until the man screamed, heat spread between their bellies. Crave swallowed the yell, and sunk his teeth into Twitch's trembling lower lip. He increased his pace until he roughly rutted as he felt the tingling at the base of his spine, his ass muscled clenched, and he thrust one last time until he emptied into the condom. A sound of possession and release rumbled in his chest, and he fisted Twitch's silky hair in his hands. He rode out the mind-shattering ecstasy, then he collapsed on Twitch, barely catching himself to keep most of his weight off Twitch.

Soft fingertips traced patterns on his back and Twitch panted beneath him.

"I have a complaint."

"Oh yeah, and what the fuck would that be?"

"No shower."

"Don't like my scent on you."

"Shut up, you know I do, why do you think I stole your shirts all the damn time?"

Now, the truth came out, and it was a hell of a lot better than he thought. "I just figured you liked my clothes," Crave teased.

"Whatever, now where the fuck are the wet wipes."

"We don't need them, we have a whole lake to swim in and a new experience for you."

"Oh, and what might that be?"

"Skinny dipping, and outside sex."

"Yes, please."

He easily slipped his arm beneath Twitch, reached back with the other to unzip the tent flap, and crawled backward out. Crave got to his feet, gently lifted Twitch off his cock, and removed the condom, and he tossed it into the still burning fire. He took off running toward the lake, Twitch laughing in his arms and he realized it wouldn't get much better than that—no fucking way, he finally had his man, and he was keeping him.

20 IT'S JUST A RING OR IS IT?

Three months passed, they'd move Nettie into her little house, and she was doing great. She still lost herself when she became tired, but they had more good days than bad. Crave and he spent every free minute they had with her. Harper was doing fantastic with her, and Harper even seemed happier.

It was technically Crave and his four-month anniversary. He clicked open the black velvet jeweler's box. Two rings were nestled in the smooth, purple fabric. Twitch had thought about it since the night they'd spent out at the lake. He didn't know if he wanted the whole ceremony or whatever, it's just a ring, right?

He felt the lie deep in his belly, it wasn't just a ring, but they hadn't talked about marriage. He knew Crave still held back, not in his declarations of love or his promises that Twitch was it for him, although, marriage wasn't mentioned.

Twitch backed up until the backs of his knees hit the mattress, and he sat on the edge. Studying the two black bands, one Crave's size and his significantly smaller. He stroked his thumb over the cool metal.

Twitch arranged to have the house to themselves tonight. Crave worked it out months ago that they'd have the same day off. Hunter, Bull, and Psycho were crashing at Tank's cabin tonight and would be home in time to get ready for work.

He'd cooked Crave's favorite dinner and dessert, queued up a blood and guts action movie. Not Twitch's type of movie, he was more of a reader, but Crave liked to cuddle him on the couch. He could deal with one of Crave's movies for that.

"What the fuck, you can't answer the door no more," Lucky barked from behind him.

Twitch jerked his head around to find Lucky standing framed by the doorway.

"Shit, I didn't even hear, what you doing here?"

"Since you've been attached to the Neanderthal, we don't see much of you. You're making my Pretty Bear worry."

"I'm sorry."

"Don't be fucking sorry."

He tracked Lucky until the man sat on the floor with his legs crossed. Lucky looked up at him.

"Listen, don't get me fucking wrong, but Crave ain't exactly the partner I would've picked for you. He's impulsive, poor impulse control, and don't forget his issues with his temper, but…" Lucky took a breath and motioned to the ring box, "It seems you see something the rest of us don't."

"He's nice to me."

"Other men would be nice too."

Twitch sighed, and combed his fingers through his hair. "It's more than that, Lucky. He gets me. I don't have to smile and pretend I'm normal when I'm breaking down."

"That's all fucking well and good, Twitch, but this is your first...sexual relationship. Shouldn't you take a few dicks for a test ride before shackling yourself to one?"

"Why aren't you happy for me?"

"I am, but it's fucking Crave, literally."

Twitch snorted. "Did you give Priest the same advice?"

"Fuck no! Shit, okay, okay, listen, I'm just saying, maybe..."

"I've tried. I couldn't even get to the kissing stage. I feel safe, don't you get that?"

"I do, but being with someone with a background like yours and Priest's take a lot of understanding. A shit ton of patience. No matter how fucking great you think you're doing, one day it's gonna blindside ya."

"I get that. It's never going to be perfect. I'm not a kid. I know what I want."

"I just want you to be sure, Twitch. This...I try every day to make sure Priest feels safe and secure, to know he can break, and it won't change how I feel about him."

"Are you saying Crave can't do that for me," Twitch asked, then nervously nibbled his bottom lip.

He closed the box with a click of the hinge. He stroked his fingertips and thumbs over the fabric. Lucky only wanted what was best for him and Twitch understood it, but he didn't have doubts when it came to Crave. He didn't want to fight with his friends just to prove Crave made him happy.

"Twitch." Lucky raised his hands and placed them on Twitch's knees.

"What?"

"If you're sure, if you've got no fucking doubts whatsoever, then that's great. I'll support you. I love you, Priest loves you, you know that, Twitch. And whatever you decide to do with those beautiful rings we'll support you."

"You don't think I'm fucking up?"

Lucky sighed. "Not my place to say, why don't you ask him." Lucky lifted his right hand and pointed to the door.

He glanced over his shoulder to find Crave with his shoulder leaned against the door frame. Crave's expression was unreadable. Shit, that was never good. He turned in time to see Lucky standing in front of him. The leanly muscled man bent down to brush a kiss against his cheek, then Lucky straightened and headed for the door.

Twitch's gaze followed Lucky, and overheard Lucky telling Crave not to fuck up before he disappeared around Crave's larger form.

"Shit," Twitch groaned and raised his hands to cover his face.

A calloused hand circled his wrists and tugged, but he refused to look at Crave.

"Come on, baby, let me see those beautiful eyes," Crave's whispered.

Twitch slowly exhaled as Crave's firm mouth pressed to his, gently nipping at his lower lip.

"I don't wanna."

Crave chuckled. "Twitch, please."

Dammit, Crave's softly spoken please always got him. He tilted his head and open his eyes to take in Crave's handsome smile.

"Do you doubt me?"

"Of course not. You're an asshole, but that's…"

"You could've stopped with the of course not."

"Yeah, but you being an asshole is true."

"What's," Crave tapped the small box, "this?"

Twitch deeply inhaled, then exhaled slowly. "I was more confident before…"

"Forget that hyper hippie bastard, just say it."

"I know we haven't been together long." Twitch open the box never taking his gaze off Crave. He wanted to see the man's reaction. Crave's expression never changed. "We never discussed, you know, getting married, and, to be honest, I'm not sure if I want the whole ceremony and all. I wanted us to, fuck, this was stupid." He lowered his chin to his chest.

"Shut up."

Twitch lifted his head as he felt Crave's hand nudge his chin.

"What this is between us, is just us," Crave's tone gentled as he spoke. "So, what's going on in your head?"

"You know what's going on in my head."

"I want you to ask me, though."

Crave's smirk caused him to narrow his eyes.

"I think I changed my mind."

"No, you haven't, ask me."

"Crave, will you…" Twitch cleared his throat, his nervousness and panic began to take over, "will you marry me?" He lifted the small box.

"Yes."

"Yes?" He resisted the urge to squeal and threw his arms around Crave's neck.

Crave's strong arms tightly wrapped around him. He held his breath as Crave retreated, his scruffy cheek stroking across Twitch's smoother one. He squeezed his eyes shut as warm breath fanned across his mouth. Crave kissed him tenderly, gentle nips and sucks at his lips. Crave's nose bumped his until Twitch opened his eyes.

"Yes, can we sort of say I asked you?"

"No, I'm telling everyone I asked."

Crave's eyes rolled. "Of course you will. You going to put it on me?"

He observed Crave sitting back on his heels. Twitch's hands shook when he tried to remove Crave's ring. He finally slipped it free and Crave held out his hand. He slowly slid the ring onto Crave's finger.

"I'll make sure you never regret this. I love you. It fucking amazes me every day I wake up with you curled up to me. You have to promise me something, though."

He knew what Crave was going to say and he wasn't going to let Crave's doubts get in the way. "You won't, you'd never put your hands on me in anger. I'm not sure about a lot of things, but I'm positive about that."

Crave's hands bracketed his face, and the kiss was soft and slow. Tears started to slip from the corners of his eyes and left warm, wet trails down his cheeks. He pushed into the kiss, and it intensified as he felt the cool metal of the second ring sliding onto his finger. His heart pounded in his chest, and as Crave broke the kiss, Twitch tried to catch his breath.

The man's large hand took Twitch's hand and lifted his to his mouth. Crave's kissed the ring never taking his gaze from Twitch's face.

"I love you, thank you for thinking I'm not broken."

"Baby, you were never broken, maybe slightly bent, and I love everything about you. Wanna quickie before the guys come home and complain about your beautiful screams?"

"Actually, I arranged for them not to come back tonight."

Crave crowded him until Twitch laid back on the bed with Crave hovered over him.

"Best fucking plan ever."

EPILOGUE: IT'S A TWIRLED BABY!

"I want fucking drugs, you sadistic fucks," Lou, Lucky's sister, screamed from the hospital bed.

Her body contorted and Crave's stomach attempted to turn inside out. What the hell was he doing here? He pressed his back against the wall and wished he could disappear through it. Twitch stood next to the bed tightly holding onto Lou's hand.

The room was packed with the Twirled Crew. Apparently, they'd decided on a birthing center so everyone could experience the so-called miracle of birth, since it was the first baby born in their functional, dysfunctional family. Crave was horrified by it.

"I'm not doing this shit again." Lou's growl turned into a scream, "He'll be an only child, you fuckers!"

He wondered why she did it in the first fucking place.

The midwife flipped the sheet up. "Aw, fuck naw!" He jerked around so fast he nearly fell on his face.

"Such a fucking man." Lily smacked the back of his head as she passed him heading for the bed. "Lou, breathe and quick screaming. It's like you're the first woman to have a damn baby."

"I want…"

"No fucking drugs, I'm not losing the damn bet."

"What bet," Lou yelled.

"Linus bet me a hundred you'd break, woman up. I ain't losing."

"Linus!"

"She's talking shit, I got two hundred that you'd squeeze your legs together and try to escape to the nearest pharmacy. I'll call him Conehead. It's gonna be the ugliest parasite ever born."

"My son is gonna be gorgeous, you're gonna end up in the morgue, motherfucker," Lucky growled from his spot beside the bed.

"Whatever you say, man. Let's hope like fuck it looks like Priest."

"He better."

Lou's scream made Crave cringe and his stomach twisted into a tighter knot. He jerked his gaze toward the door and wondered if anyone would notice if he escaped. Crave knew he'd never live it down. Especially with Bull sitting casually in the corner with a bored expression on his face.

Crave barely paid attention to the argument going on behind him. He focused on the sweet sound of Twitch's voice as his man attempted to soothe the pissed and in pain Lou. He did notice something interesting, Linus winced along with every curse and scream that passed Lou's lips.

"Did we miss it," Elijah asked as he busted through the door with Scary and Tank close behind.

Fucking great, more people. He took a few steps and spun to press his back against the wall. He tried to look everywhere but at the bed.

"Lou, you're fully dilated, you ready," the midwife's voice was calm, almost a monotone.

"Do I look fucking ready?"

Lou's question drew his attention. Her dark blonde, purple streaked hair stuck to her sweaty face. Her normally tanned complexion was a mottled red. Tears leaked from the corners of her pain-filled eyes. Lou looked exhausted.

Twitch was gently stroking her hair, and she was leaned into his touch. A small smile tilted the corners of Twitch's lush lips.

It hit him again that the beautiful man was his. Crave twisted the ring on his left hand.

"Okay, Lou, on the next contraction I want you to push. Just listen to your body."

Lucky pressed his body close to Priest's from behind. The hyper hippie's mouth brushed Priest's throat as Priest held Lou's left hand while Twitch held the other.

"Do we got a damn baby yet?" Psycho busted into the room, grunting as he looked toward the bed.

Psycho shook his head as he approached Crave.

"Not gonna puke, are ya?"

"No, I'm not gonna puke," Crave answered with no confidence.

Surrounded by his friends, chosen family, time became measured in long drawn out grunts, heavy panting, and curses that would make a seasoned biker blush. He shuddered as Twitch and Priest were asked to practically bend Lou in half.

The midwife moved to the side to grab a towel and exposed the horror, nausea built from the pit of his stomach up through his esophagus, and the burning began at the back of his throat. A head of hair matted down by blood and unknown substances slipped free. Crave's vision began to dim at the edges, he fought it, but the next thing he knew he was falling.

"Man down," Psycho barked out with a booming laugh.

A cry rang out, and everything went black as a muffled voice called, "Congratulations, it's a boy!"

THE END

ABOUT THE AUTHOR

By day, J.M. is an introverted cook hiding out in her kitchen in the middle of nowhere Ohio, by night and any free time she may have, she is a writer of mainly LGBTQ Fiction and Erotica. Although. she's equal opportunity when it comes to telling a story, she'll even write a bit of straight erotic romance when the mood strikes.

She has been writing for years in old notebooks. At the age of eight, she wrote the worst poem in the history of poetry, but it sparked her love for writing. She reads too much and loves to get lost in other worlds and her favorite stories have to include laughter and having the reader doing at least one double take. Thirty-something, forever restless she uses her stories to ground herself, and find her place of peace.

WHERE TO FIND J.M.
www.jmdabneyauthor.com

AVAILABLE NOW

PSYCHO
Brawlers 2

Welcome to Brawlers Bar…

Life wasn't easy when you were certifiable, Gerald "Psycho" Clemons lived on the fringes of society. For five years, he hadn't thought twice about riding with a group who saw most laws as flexible. When the leader of the group turned crazier than Psycho, he stepped in and made the man pay. He'd never been rewarded for his temper before, yet that's what happened when he earned a permanent place and a job as a bouncer. Everyone walked a wide circle around him, and he liked it that way. One look from his cold black eyes and he had people backing up. Then he met a man who had to be crazier than him.

Decadence Bakery was Ben Morin's dream come true, and he loved it, but he grew tired of his lonely existence. Six months earlier he'd turned on the open sign and hopefully changed his life for the better. Ben loved his small cottage in the middle of nowhere even with the 3 a.m. rumbling of motorcycles and loud music at the farm next door. Although one thing he didn't love was his new hobby of watching one of the terrifying men next door. What could a little harmless peek every now and then hurt?

Sweet and older wasn't his type, but Psycho couldn't deny the need to possess the beautiful baker. It was stronger than even the insanity he barely kept at bay. Could he have a man who looked passed it or would Ben run like all the rest?

■■■■

1 MOTHERFUCKER, WHERE ARE YOUR MEDS?

Lean perfection strolled through the thinning crowd of scarred leather and dirty boots with a grace that put all men to shame. Fuck, he wanted a pretty fucker like that, Elijah Davis-Sheridan belonged to his bosses, but he'd trailed Elijah for months studying the man. What the hell had two rough sons of bitches like Scary and Tank done to earn Elijah? Gerald Clemons aka Psycho still couldn't figure that shit out.

"The bosses are going to get the wrong idea if you keep checking out their husband."

He turned his head to find Twitch, the pretty little bartender, watching him with his pointed chin resting on top his laced fingers. Crave, Brawlers' head of security, had gotten the sweet little man and Crave was a bigger asshole than him. What the fuck was he doing wrong?

"Elijah is my responsibility."

"You know Eli doesn't need his own security, right?"

"Of course he does, look at him, what bastard wouldn't—"

"Don't get a hard-on for Scary and Tank's man, I really kinda like you."

"Why?"

"Why what?"

"Like me?"

"You're kinda sweet in a socially awkward psychotic sort of way."

No one ever thought he was sweet before. Twitch was small and delicate—beautiful—he didn't do well with those things. He looked down at his scarred hands with the rough, calloused knuckles from years of fighting. Psycho wasn't gentle. His voice was as rough as his exterior with a gravelly, dangerous tone, it wasn't sweet or soothing.

He'd listened to Scary talk to Elijah, Crave to Twitch, and their men just seemed to relax. He was fucked, and he didn't want to be, he wanted a man that actually liked him for shit other than his dick. Even though he had to admit that monster was fucking impressive. He was getting distracted.

"Is that something men like, sweet?" He felt his snarl and sensed that wasn't the right reaction. It was going to be harder than he first thought.

"You don't have to say it like it's disgusting. Not all men—"

"But what are sweet things," Psycho laid his forearms on the bar and leaned forward.

"I don't know dates—"

"I can do dates, what else?"

"Psycho, this is all pretty—"

"What else?" He grimaced as he raised his voice. *Bad Psycho*, he mentally yelled at himself.

"Calm down, damn, okay, let's see, doing things for a person you care about?"

"Like what?"

"Have you ever been on a date?"

"I used to take my ex-wife on dates. Bernie liked pizza and beer, improving her accuracy as a sniper. That woman had a mean fucking aim. It was fucking beautiful."

Bernie was just as fucking vicious as him. She'd rather throw down against a man three times her size than do all that shit chicks like to do. They were both bi, but she leaned more toward women while he was more interested in fucking men.

They hadn't loved each other in a romantic way. They both grew up in the same crew. No one fucking knew what right was and useless things such as consciences were beaten out of them early. They'd skipped out of their hometown together. They hadn't parted ways until a few years ago when Bernie hooked up with a pretty little waitress down in Texas.

"Okay, let me ask you this. Is it someone like Elijah you're looking for or maybe someone like—"

"Elijah. I mean, I'm just like them. I'm an asshole. I've made grown men piss themselves, I'm fucking terrifying and I can't...what the fuck am I doing wrong?"

"Maybe you're just trying too hard."

"What the fuck are you talking about?"

"You're tagging along after Elijah to do recon to figure out what Scary and Tank did to earn him, right?"

"Yeah, but he also needs someone to watch his back."

"You may think so, but I'm sure Elijah can take care of himself."

"He got himself kidnapped and then taunted the crazy fucker, the man ain't...oh, he ain't right, is he?"

"Elijah is fine, he complements Scary and Tank, and they do the same to him. Two similar people in the same relationship—"

"Fight."

"Maybe, but you need someone who makes everything calm. Soothes the chaos storming inside you."

"Is that what Crave does for you, calms you? Shouldn't fucking be involved?"

"Yes, sex is important, but Crave grounds me when things get to be too much in my head. He brings me back."

"This is so fucking confusing."

"You want a beer?"

"And a shot, make it a double, make it two."

Twitch's laughter was almost musical. He hadn't heard it much before the man hooked up with Crave. Would he do that for a man? He didn't see how it was possible. Psycho was a hard man. He'd literally fought for survival and dominance since he understood hierarchy. The meanest fucker won, and the weakest licked someone's fucking boots.

He observed Twitch as the man set him up with two rock glasses with doubles of top shelf bourbon and a dark perspiring bottle. Twitch left him alone with his thoughts. He wasn't going to find one of those elusive men in a place like Brawlers. Sure, he could find a fuck easy enough, but he could get the same with a good jerk off session. Best thing is afterward he didn't have to kick some trick out of his bed.

He downed the two doubles in quick succession and chased it with the ice-cold beer. The liquor warmed his stomach and chest, then the beer eased it. What was he supposed to do? He worked at Brawlers five nights a week, took long rides on his bike in his free time and that's it. He hung out with guys he worked with and considered friends. Bernie had been his only friend before he'd moved there.

Psycho didn't live in the house with the guys, Bull let him move a trailer behind the barn. He'd gotten used to his space. Too many years of camping out on a bedroll between towns with whoever he was riding with at the time. Cheap motels came in handy for cold nights or hookups. He slid the glasses to the bar rail for Twitch to wash. Last call was coming up, and then they'd be headed out while Scary and Tank handled the accounting shit.

"Psycho, you're quieter than normal."

He turned to see Elijah take the stool next to his and smile up at him. Elijah's head was tilted slightly as the man studied him. Sometimes he wondered if Elijah thought of him as a project, but then he shook off the thought. Elijah didn't possess a hardened edge or a mean bone in his body. He wasn't saying Elijah couldn't throw down when his husbands or daughter, Juvie, were in danger. It just took a lot to make the man lose his temper.

"Just thinking."

"About what?"

"Stupid shit," Psycho didn't want to go into it. He'd already tried the advice thing with Twitch, and it left him baffled.

"Come on, Psycho, talk to me." Elijah reached out and pushed his bicep.

"I don't know how to date."

"Of course you don't, you've never had to do it before. I've met Bernie, and she's as hard as you, she didn't seem like the romantic date type. So, what're you going to do about it?"

"Nothing," He answered.

"Bullshit, you're around men all the time, one of them had to have caught your attention."

"Nope." He found plenty of men he'd fuck, but none he'd want to date or even take the time to try.

"Okay, then what are you looking for?"

"I don't know, someone like you. Scary and Tank got you, and they're—"

Elijah cut him off with a chuckle.

"I love my men. All the rough edges and all, but you're not exactly approachable."

"Why?"

"Psycho, you scowl all the time. I've never seen you smile beyond one of your micro-smiles."

He felt the corner of his mouth lift.

"See, you should do that more often and for a little longer."

"Smile, check, what else?"

"Maybe go places in town instead of hanging out here."

"Like where?"

"I don't know, maybe take a ride around town. I know you like to read. There's that new bakery next to Nightingale's Books. Juvie loves their cinnamon rolls."

"Go places, check, what—"

"Don't worry about it so much. You're stressing. You're weird, but you're not that bad. I think you may even be a catch."

"Really, ready to leave—"

Elijah laughed, and two pissed off growls joined it.

Psycho glanced behind Elijah to find Scary and Tank watching Psycho with murder in their eyes.

"I don't poach."

"We're starting to doubt that. Baby, you ready to go home and enjoy the rest of the night without our little chaperon?"

"Definitely," Elijah whispered and leaned forward to brush Psycho's cheek with his soft, full lips. "You'll find him, Psycho, I'm sure of it."

"Thanks, Elijah."

"No problem," Elijah spun and before he could stand, both Scary and Tank reached for Elijah.

Psycho watched the way the guy melted into his men. Again, he couldn't find or keep one man, and there were men who'd found two men to love them. Psycho was jealous as fuck. He turned back to his beer as the three men walked off and he was left alone. Crave was leaned across the bar sharing a kiss with a blushing Twitch. Bull was at the end opposite him staring into a double whiskey neat he never drank. Hunter was curled up in a booth on his phone doing whatever Hunter did.

He dropped his gaze to his bottle and slowly peeled the label as he rethought his original plan. Maybe it just wasn't meant to be, and he was dreaming of the impossible. Psycho lifted the bottle to his mouth, drained the last of it, and set it on the rail. He didn't bother to say goodbye when he stood and headed for the door. A long ride is what he needed, he didn't have work tomorrow, so he didn't have to be home anytime soon. Home—was this fucking place home or was it time to move on again?

■■■■

He decided to take Elijah's advice and get out. Nightingale's was a funky little shop off the main drag on a side street that housed a weird combination of restaurants and shops including Twirled World Ink.

Psycho walked the aisles and grabbed random books, turned them over and read the back covers. He liked to read. He'd spent so much time alone he'd developed a habit of picking up a book or two in every town he passed through. It had been a month or two since he'd visited the store. A flash of pink shimmered in his peripheral, and he turned his head to find Harper slowly walking toward him.

Her long, honey blonde hair was pulled into a messy bun on the top of her head. He gave her a small smile. She wore her usual style of flowing dresses, but it didn't have the usual flowers, but a pale pink one that fell all the way to the floor.

"Hi, Psycho, haven't seen you in a while."

Harper's voice held a musical and husky tone, it was like something you'd hear from some old timed blues singer. She was delicate and sweet, he'd almost asked her out a time or two when he first moved there.

The woman had a hard time of it. Being the only openly Transwoman in town drew bigger bullies faster than shit drew flies.

"Kinda keep myself busy out at Brawlers."

"Yeah, Crave and Twitch have some crazy stories when they visit Nettie."

Harper had nursing experience but hadn't found a nursing job in Powers. When Twitch and Crave moved Crave's mother Nettie to town, they'd hired Harper to sit with the woman part-time.

"Why don't you come out one night?"

Harper shook her head, "Oh, Psycho, I don't think—"

He knew what she was going to say. Brawlers was the only gay bar in Powers, but really a lot of women came out on the weekends. Lily and Peaches, Bernie and Stacey were regulars when they made it to town.

"Maybe on a night Lily and Peaches come, you can hang out with them and the Twirled Crew. I'd keep an eye on you."

"I appreciate that, Psycho, and I'll think about."

He didn't want to push. Harper was skittish. He shot a quick glance at her wrists with the wide cuffs and noticed a bandage peeking from beneath the faux leather. Instead of opening his mouth and demanding answers, he focused on the book in his hand.

They all tried to help. Twitch invited her to lunch or out to the farm, but Harper tended to be more reclusive than him.

"Have you tried the new bakery next door?"

"No, Elijah mentioned it the other night. He said I needed to get out more."

"You can't kick ass and take names twenty-four-seven, Psycho."

"But what if I'm really good at it?"

He liked when she smiled. Harper didn't do it enough. One of the members of the Executioners who played Brawlers a few times a month kept an eye on her. Joker made sure he kept people from fucking with her too much. That man had to be crazier than him which was saying a lot.

"I've watched you in the ring before. I thought you and Bull were going to kill each other."

"Naw, we're good."

"Well, it was fun, I might take Twitch up on his offer of coming out next time."

"Do that."

"Well, since Elijah wants you to get out, I'd definitely stop in at Decadence. I swear I could live on that man's coffee."

"Got yourself a crush?"

Her pale cheeks pinkened, and he shook his head. Even with the horror stories he'd heard, it still surprised him when he saw the woman blush.

"Not on him just his coffee. He really isn't my type."

"I think I'm going to get these and head over for coffee, you want one?"

"That's so sweet, but I just grabbed one before I came in. Come on, I'll ring you up."

She turned away and walked out of the aisle. He followed at a distance. Psycho didn't like anyone at his back, and he sensed Harper didn't either. Harper rang him up, and he offered another invite to Brawlers, even said he'd come out and get her. He'd noticed her longingly staring at the crew's bikes a time or two. She answered with a maybe, and he said bye, he exited the shop and turned left to check out the new bakery.

www.ingramcontent.com/pod-product-compliance
Lightning Source LLC
Chambersburg PA
CBHW060152130626
46556CB00006B/2612